RAY

DIVISION

A Carefree Novel

DIVISION: A Carefree Novel

ISBN-13: 9798393435196

Copyright © 2023 by Leslie Ray

Cover Design: Leslie Ray of Digital Design Studio

www.LeslieRayAuthor.com

Other great titles by Leslie Ray

The Carefree Series
EXPOSURE
UNEXPECTED
DIVISION
Book 4 (Coming Soon)
Book 5 (Coming Soon)

The Spruce Pine Series
RUN TO ME
FORGIVE ME

Don't miss out! Join my newsletter for exclusive content, giveaways, updates, and more at LeslieRayAuthor.com

Follow me on social media
@LeslieRayAuthor

Chapter One

All evening, Liam Scott watched his past float around the wedding reception like an elegant swan. Beneath the glow of the Edison lights, strung across the open patio, she moved with grace and poise, attending to every detail.

For five months and three days—not that he was counting—he'd dreamt of what it would be like to see Stella James after all these years, but not a single one of those dreams was living up to the reality. Like a fine wine, she'd aged to perfection. Her soft lips, twisted up in a smile, were fuller than he remembered. As were the curves snaking up her body.

And damn if her long auburn hair, hanging over her shoulder like a sin, wasn't beckoning him to run his fingers through it.

It was funny thinking back to the phone call from his now sister-in-law. Julia wanted to tell him up front that she and Miles, Liam's oldest brother, were getting married at Pebble Creek Plantation. The event venue owned by his ex-fiancé. He'd assured Julia it wouldn't be a problem, but now, watching Stella's hips sway as she moved through the crowd, it felt like he'd signed his own death warrant.

The last time he'd been in the same space as his ex, things had gone off the rails in a hurry. A lot of angry words had been said that day. Words he'd spent a lot of time wishing he could take back.

But that was the thing about the past, no one could change it.

Looking back, he couldn't blame Stella for staying in South Carolina. He'd been young and wild, with a burning need to run free. Stella on the other hand had goals and plans. And based on his surroundings, those goals and plans had landed her right in the middle of success.

"You know they're taking bets on how long it takes you to crash and burn?"

Liam looked up to find his very pregnant sister standing over him. "I don't know what you're talking about?"

"I'm sure you don't." Kat eased herself down into the chair beside him. "I'm sure you haven't noticed Stella in her form-fitting black dress either?"

"Nope." He was a damn liar, and Kat knew it. Picking up the bottle of beer he'd been nursing for the last half hour, Liam took a long draw. "I'm just here for the free beer."

"Ah, I miss beer, and having a body like that." Kat rubbed a hand across her swollen belly, and nodded in Stella's direction.

"I can't help with the beer or the body, but what would you say to a spin on the dance floor?" Placing his bottle back on the table, Liam stood and held out his hand. He needed the distraction more than he cared to admit.

"If by spin you mean waddle, then I'm good for at least three minutes before I have to pee or pass out. But first, you're going to have to pull me out of this chair."

For the next two hours, Liam alternated between twirling the women in his family around the dance floor, and laughing with his brothers. After twelve years of living in Colorado, being back in Carefree felt good. He didn't have a damn clue what he was going to do with the abundance of free time now that his plate was empty, but for the moment he enjoying the ride.

Until last fall, Liam hadn't realized how much he missed being with family or his quaint little hometown. Coming back had meant giving up a lot, but standing in the middle of his brother's reception, surrounded by all his siblings, it was worth the sacrifice.

As the party began to wind down, Liam caught himself searching for the one woman he hadn't worked up the nerve to speak to yet. The crowd had thinned to mostly family and their closest friends, but Stella was nowhere to be found. She'd been so attentive the entire evening, he couldn't imagine her leaving before the reception was over. Pulling out his phone, he glanced at the time, shocked to see it was almost eleven.

The DJ's voice boomed through the mic. "We're going to slow it down for one last dance for the bride and groom."

Slipping his phone back in his pocket, Liam smiled as his sister and brother-in-law approached. "You're not giving up now, are you?"

Kat waddled her way toward him, her sandals dangling from her hand. "I'm pretty sure I have exceeded my activity level for the next month. Besides, I didn't want to steal the spotlight from the happy couple." Glancing over her shoulder, Liam followed her line of sight back to the dance floor where Miles and Julia were swaying to the slow music.

Other than the newlyweds, the floor had cleared out. All around them, the remaining guests were collecting their belongings, while staff began clearing the unoccupied tables. "Do we need to do anything to help out?"

"No, Stella said she would collect all of our decorations, and drop them by the diner next week." Kat grabbed her stuff from the table and turned toward the exit. "Come on, we saved some sparklers for their real exit."

Earlier in the evening, the photographer had staged a fake exit, photographing Miles and Julia leaving under an archway of glowing sparklers. It had seemed kind of ridiculous to Liam given they weren't actually leaving, but he wasn't surprised Kat had saved some. "I'm right behind you."

Liam glanced around the staff milling about hoping to catch a glimpse of Stella, but as far as he could see, she'd yet to reappear. Grabbing his coat from the back of the chair, he pulled his phone from his pants pocket, and tossed it on the table. It was a stupid idea, but it was the best he could do for now.

When he reached the front of the plantation house, his family was lined up along the walkway. Stopping at the end of the line, he took the unlit sparkler, and lighter from Kat.

"As soon as they come around, we need to light them as fast as we can." Kat barely got the words out of her mouth when Miles and Julia appeared. "Okay, go. Hurry up."

Holding the tiny fireworks up once again, everyone began to cheer as the couple made their way through the makeshift archway to Miles's truck. With the scent of magnesium lingering in the air, they all waved goodbye as the truck disappeared down the driveway.

Kat let out a loud yawn. "I don't know about the rest of you, but I may sleep for the next two days."

Brooks, Kat's husband of a few months, pulled her to his side. "That's the most fun I've had in a long time."

"The most fun you've had in a long time, huh?" Kat twisted her face up toward her husband.

"Aside from all things pertaining to you, of course."

Liam felt a pang of jealousy twist his stomach as Brooks leaned down and placed a soft kiss on Kat's forehead. It made sense Kat and Miles would be the first two siblings to get married since they were the oldest, but if they were going in order Liam was next in line, and he couldn't remember the last time he'd had a decent date, much less a serious relationship.

Well, that wasn't entirely true. He knew exactly when his last serious relationship ended.

As the group slowly worked their way toward the parking area, Liam stopped, and patted his pockets for show. "I must have left my phone on the table."

"Do you want us to come help you find it?" Kat was already turning back toward the house when Brooks wrapped his arm around her.

His brother-in-law's lips twisted into a knowing smile. "I think Liam can handle it."

Busted. So much for pretending he had left his phone by accident.

"Brooks is right, I just need to run back, and grab it. Plus, you're already exhausted. I'll see you guys tomorrow." Liam hugged his sister goodnight.

If he was going to crash and burn, he didn't need an audience.

*****

Stella James was a lot of things, but remaining levelheaded when it came to Liam Scott was not one of them. Standing in her dimly lit office inside the old mansion, she was pretty proud of herself for maintaining her professionalism as long as she had, but she wasn't a saint. Hence the bottle of pinot she'd swiped from the bar that was now empty.

It had been twelve years since she'd laid eyes on all six feet, one inch of her ex. Unfortunately for her, however, Liam had only grown more handsome with the years. Every inch of him was pure perfection. At least, she was guessing based on the lean frame under the well-tailored suit, clean cut, and fresh shave. Thanks to the old memories she'd tried so hard to forget, her brain happily filled in the blanks of what was under the vest and tie.

A few times, as she'd scanned the reception, she'd caught his piercing green eyes studying her. She'd been careful not to make eye contact, but knowing he was watching her had set her blood to boil. Precisely the reason she was now hiding in her dark office, waiting for all the guests to leave.

The book of Liam Scott was closed. The story finished. No matter how appealing he may be or how lacking her love life had been lately, the last thing she needed was to crack open those pages again.

Glancing out the front window, Stella watched as the last of the sparklers went out and the Scott clan moved toward their vehicles. Once upon a very long time ago, she was certain she would be a part of their family, but it had only been an illusion.

Maybe it was the wine talking, but a part of her wanted to march out there, and demand answers to the questions she'd been wondering for years. For starters, if Liam hadn't wanted to marry her, why had he asked in the first place? Why bother putting a ring on her finger and continuing a charade he had no intention of following through on?

The disillusion had been the hardest part.

No one had forced him to ask for her hand in marriage. He'd asked of his own free will, and she'd said yes, happily, because everything had seemed perfect. Then he'd pulled the rug out from under her feet. Stella had never taken Liam to be a cruel man...until that day.

She'd cried for what felt like a month, hoping every new dawn would be the day he changed his mind, and came home. But with every sunset, her hope had dwindled a little more. He never called. Never wrote. It was as though she'd never existed.

It had taken her a long time to accept the hard truth that Liam Scott wasn't the man she'd believed him to be.

With the Scott family on their way, Stella let out the breath she'd been holding all evening. Liam would go back to Colorado, and she would go back to pretending he didn't exist.

The end.

Slipping off her heels, Stella weaved her way back through the mansion, out the back door, and down the steps to where her staff was clearing tables. Thanks to the pinot, her head was feeling a little lighter than usual, but she only had to pull herself together enough to get through the next twenty minutes.

The tables and chairs would be fine until tomorrow, but she'd promised Julia they would collect and store the decorations until Stella could return them to Carefree. Her staff would also need to remove any remaining dinnerware and glasses before the ants took over, but from the looks of it, there was little to do where that was concerned.

Before Stella could get started, her assistant Whitney approached, holding a phone up in front of her. "Only one phone left behind, not bad considering the amount of alcohol this group consumed."

Lost items were not a rarity around the plantation. It seemed someone was always leaving something behind. Phones were usually reclaimed the next day when their owner sobered up enough to realize it was missing. As for all the other lost items, they generally lived in her office closet for six months before being donated to a local thrift store.

"I'll put it with the decorations. I'm sure the bride's sister-in-law will know who it belongs to if the owner doesn't come to claim it first."

"Sounds good."

As her assistant handed over the phone, the lock screen lit up, revealing a photo of the snowcapped Colorado Rockies. Stella's heart skipped a beat. What were the odds someone else at the wedding had a photo of the Rockies on their phone?

Curiosity joined the wine coursing through her veins. Her entire life was on her phone, which meant if this was Liam's phone, then…

Before she could stop herself, Stella swiped the screen, not surprised when it prompted her for a password. She tried the most obvious first, his birthday. No luck. With nine remaining attempts, she tried every four-digit combo she could think of, his parent's street address, even one, two, three, four. Still, no luck.

With two attempts left before the phone's data completely erased, she decided to try one last combination. It was arrogant and a long shot, but she'd tried everything else she could think of. Entering her birthday, Stella gasped when the phone unlocked.

It had to be a coincidence, right?

Suddenly, she wasn't sure if her head was swimming from the wine or the new discovery. The date had to be significant for some other reason. They hadn't spoken in over a decade. There was no way he was using her birthday as his passcode.

Except, the thought of Liam even remembering her birthday, much less using it, sent an odd thrill through her.

Stuffing the unwelcome emotion back down, Stella stared at the screen full of apps. Snooping through his personal information felt wrong on so many levels, but a drunk part of her needed to know what his life was like. Was he married, not that she'd noticed a ring? Did he have a girlfriend? Maybe a few girlfriends.

"I'm sorry." Stella whispered into the night air as she tapped the camera roll, and opened his images. Tomorrow, she'd blame it on the wine, but for tonight, she couldn't help herself.

Skimming through the photos, she was stunned to find not a single one was of a woman. The photos were all of nature, rugged trails, and mountain peaks. A few scattered throughout the roll were of different groups on the banks of a river before rafting. She had to assume those were all trips his company had guided.

As she scrolled a bit further, she came across a section that looked like some sort of home renovation project. From the exterior photos, the home was a slender, two-story Italianate style house. The interior, however, was in the process of being renovated to have a very modern feel.

"It was a lot of work, but the finished product was pretty worth it."

Stella froze. Rich cologne swirled in her nose as Liam's words drifted over her bare shoulder. Turning slowly, she took in the sight of him standing far too close.

"I was trying to see whose phone it was," she lied through a tight smile.

His eyes dropped back to the photos on his phone, as a smile spread across his lips. "It took you going all the way back to September to figure it out?"

"What?" Maybe she'd drank more than she thought because his words weren't making sense.

"Those photos." Liam pointed at his phone. "I finished the renovations last September."

Words clogged in her throat. They both knew exactly what she was up to, yet she wasn't about to give him the satisfaction of admitting it. "I wasn't trying to snoop."

His light chuckle sent a shiver across her skin. "Of course not. So, how many tries did it take you to figure out the passcode?"

Well crap!

In the still of the night, the truth lingered between them. He was still holding on to a small part of them, too.

Chapter Two

Caught between a rock and a hard place, Stella stared at the phone resting in her palm, unsure of how to respond. The man who'd ripped her heart out, and fled halfway across the country twelve years ago, was using her birthday as his passcode. And damn if the little nugget of information wasn't doing all sorts of things to her mind, body, and spirit.

Especially, her mind.

It was four simple numbers, and yet somehow, they'd caused an electrical short in her brain. She could have sworn she told her feet to move, to put some distance between herself and Liam, but the signal wasn't getting through. The only thing she could manage was impersonating a slightly drunk mannequin.

As for her body and spirit, she was trying her damnedest to ignore the effect Liam had on those.

By some small miracle, Stella found her voice. "I pressed a few random numbers and it unlocked. Like I said, I was just trying to see if I could tell who the phone belonged to."

A sinister smile twisted the corners of his mouth. "You always were a terrible liar."

Liam wasn't wrong. She knew eight-year-olds with a better poker face than hers when she was stone cold sober. Since lying her way out of the situation was off the table, Stella decided to go with another tactic. Avoidance.

"It's getting late, and I need to help my staff finish packing up for the night." As she held the phone out, Liam's fingers grazed her skin, setting every nerve ending ablaze like a California wildfire. The tingling sensation rippled its way through her body, straight to the center of her self-preservation.

Without permission, fading memories of Liam's fingertips skimming her most intimate parts assaulted her mind. The memory was specific. It was the last night they'd been together. The night before everything changed. The raging summer storm had knocked out the power, leaving them with nothing but time and their bodies as entertainment. Skin to skin, they'd practically melted into one as the rain pounded against the windowpane.

"Stella?"

Glancing up, Stella watched Liam's beautiful face distort into an odd mix of emotion. Eyes slightly squinted, head tilted, he looked almost confused. Or was it concern twisting his features?

"What? Why are you looking at me like that?" The words rushed across her lips, more clipped than her usual sweet tone. Between the onslaught of memories, Liam's closeness, and fermented grapes, she was having a hard time keeping her perfected professionalism in check.

Liam's brow arched. "Well, I asked you a question, and you stood there like a statue. I was trying to determine if you were having a seizure or stroke."

Stella drew in a deep breath, determined to get herself in check. "I'm fine. I was thinking about something I need to do."

Stay far away from you is what I need to do.

As though he sensed her internal struggle, and was determined to push her closer to the edge, Liam slipped the phone into his pocket, and draped his suit coat across the back of the chair next to him. "Something I can help you with?"

Was it her imagination or had his words come out husky, and full of innuendo? "Nope, definitely not something you can help with."

Taking a step toward the next table, Stella grabbed the white tablecloth, rolled it in a ball, and held it to her chest. It was the best she could do to create a barrier between them. The last thing she needed was getting tangled up with old memories that no longer mattered.

Liam pressed forward like a pawn. "Here, let me help you with those."

"That's sweet of you to offer, really, but your brother isn't paying me top dollar so his guests can help clean up." Stella retreated, grabbing the covering from the next table and wadded it up.

She could drape every single tablecloth on the patio over her head like a ghost, and it still wouldn't be enough to block the effect he had on her. What the hell was wrong with her? Sure, he looked hotter than a Cabo beach in July, but they were old news. A thing of the past. She'd moved on.

Except, she couldn't help but wonder if it would be like riding a bike.

He's only here for the wedding and then he'll be gone…

Like a predator circling its prey, Liam stepped in closer, crowding her space. "I really don't mind helping."

If she had to guess, he knew exactly what he was doing. His sweet smile might look innocent on the surface, but she was fairly certain it had been carved by the Devil himself.

He was up to no good and it was working.

The smooth, deep sound of his voice and extreme closeness was chipping away at her resolve faster than she could convince herself that dipping her toes in the pool that was Liam Scott was a terrible idea. She needed to put some space between them before the tingling headed further south.

"I do this for a living. I promise I can handle a few tablecloths. Besides, I'm sure you have better things to do with your Saturday night."

Stella watched in disbelief as Liam stepped around her, and pulled the covering from the next table. "I'm here and I'm already helping." He held up the white fabric for emphasis. "Just point me in the right direction of where they need to go."

Why did he have to be such an insistent ass?

She couldn't have stopped her eyes from rolling if she'd wanted to. If Stella knew anything about the man standing beside her, it was how deep his determination ran. It was the reason his company was a huge success—not that she was keeping tabs on him or his business. When he had his sights set on something, he wouldn't stop until he got what he wanted.

She just needed to make sure his sights weren't set on her.

Or you could dip one toe in. He'll probably be gone by tomorrow. Her body urged her mind to get on board.

Filing the errant thought in her mental junk drawer, she did her best to redirect his attention. "Since you don't seem to understand the word no, why don't you gather the centerpieces for your sister? I told her I would drop them by the diner later this week." Stella nodded toward the table where most of the centerpieces had been gathered.

At least, if she gave him a task, she could put a little space between them. And the sooner they finished, the sooner he would leave.

"You know, I'm staying at Kat's, I can take them back if you want."

Actually, she had no idea where he was staying, and would have preferred to keep it that way. The last thing her semi-drunk mind needed to visualize was where he would be sleeping. She needed to stay focused on the task at hand. Getting Liam to leave as quickly as possible before the wine convinced her to make a few questionable choices.

"I guess it doesn't really matter who takes them back. If you want to collect what's left out here, we can box them all up together inside." The words slipped across her lips before she realized what she'd done.

As if standing beneath a blanket of stars wasn't bad enough, she'd given him a reason to stay longer. After all the blood, sweat, and tears she'd poured into Pebble Creek over the years, this place felt as intimate as her private residence, and she'd invited the big, bad wolf in.

"You're the boss, whatever you think is best."

What she thought was best was for Liam to hop on a plane, and go back to his snowcapped mountains, but she couldn't tell him that. If his consistent determination was any indication of how little he'd changed, he would take such a statement as a challenge.

And he was not one to back down from a challenge.

For the next few minutes, Stella did her best to point out items for Liam to gather while maintaining a safe distance. When both their arms were full, she took one last glance at the patio. The tables were clear and only the furniture remained. Her staff had disappeared inside the mansion, no doubt waiting for her assistant to release them for the evening.

"Anything else that needs to be done?" Liam asked as he followed her up the steps to the covered porch.

"No, you've done too much already. Everything else can wait." With her hands full, Stella tilted her head toward the door. "Come on, let's get you a box so you can be on your way."

As she stepped through the broad French doors that led into the house, her assistant appeared from the kitchen. "I sent everyone home. I was going to head out too…but I can stay if you need me to."

Stella watched as Whitney's eyes scanned up and down, assessing the man standing next to her. "Whit, this is Liam Scott. Miles and Kat's younger brother, and owner of the lost phone. We were just collecting the decorations Julia wanted to keep so he can take them back, and save me a trip to Carefree."

A knowing smile curved the corners of Whitney's lips. Though she'd never met him, Whit had heard just enough about Liam to know he was an ex. "Well, in that case, it was very nice to meet you Liam, but I'm exhausted, and my bed is calling my name." Pulling her keys from her bag, Whitney leaned in close as she passed Stella. "Don't do anything I wouldn't do."

Shocked by Whitney's not-so-quiet whisper, Stella choked out a fake cough to try and cover her assistant's words.

"Are you okay?" Liam bent down quickly, placing the load of centerpieces on the floor before coming back to her side. "Do you need some water?"

She nearly melted from the heat of his strong hand patting her gently on her back. "Actually, I think I need something stronger. I have a bottle of wine in the kitchen."

More wine was a terrible idea, but she was starting to lose her buzz, and she couldn't face him sober.

"This place is amazing."

Liam's words trailed behind her as she headed into the kitchen, and poured a tall glass of Merlot. Realizing she was being completely rude, Stella grabbed another glass, and held it out toward him. "Would you like a glass?"

"Sure. So, is it just weddings or do you do other events?" He took the glass and glanced around the full-service kitchen.

"It's an all-inclusive event space. We host everything from weddings to corporate retreats, to family reunions, and everything in between. I only book weddings two weekends out of the month." Stella launched into promotion mode.

"How exactly does that work? Having different types of events?"

"Easier than it sounds." She was starting to question her sanity, but she continued on with her answer. "Weddings are actually the hardest, well, the most exhausting. Corporate events are the easiest, and usually the most entertaining."

"How so?"

Stella drained the contents of her glass and refilled it as she spoke. "Well, it's more like a B&B or inn. Companies rent the entire property, with the exception of my office. We offer some entertainment packages if they want to do team building activities or have some fun down time. We have a large conference table in the formal dining room for meeting space, plus the patios if the weather is nice. We also have an area for lounging down here in the original living room, plus an additional space upstairs, along with eight bedrooms on the upper two levels. Most of them have two queen beds, with the exception of one that has a king."

"Eight bedrooms?"

"Yes." Stella let out a light chuckle at the surprise in his voice. The wine swirling through her head was making it easier to be around Liam than she thought. "The house originally had ten bedrooms in total, but one upstairs is now the lounging area on the second floor, and the master suite on this floor has been converted into office and storage space."

"Wow. I knew it was a big place, but damn."

Pride twisted her lips into a bright smile. "That's not counting the two small bedrooms in the boat house down on the lake."

"You up for giving a late-night tour? I'd love to see the place...if it's not too much trouble."

Stella hesitated.

The scorned woman in her didn't want to show him a single thing, but her business side couldn't help but wonder if he was considering renting the space for his own company. Things at Pebble Creek had been steady for the past few years, but business had leveled off. She hadn't seen significant growth for two years, and expanding had been on the forefront of her thoughts for months.

The sudden weight of being alone in the house with Liam pressed down on her chest. Taking another long drink of wine, Stella pulled up her proverbial big girl panties. Business was business, and she had bills to pay. If Liam wanted to book an event for his company, she wouldn't turn him down. She may not show her face while he was here, but she wouldn't turn down the money. She could do this.

"Sure, I think I have time for a quick peek."

As she led him through the house, Stella carried the bottle of wine in her hand, noting the thunder rolling in the distance. She'd kept her fingers crossed all evening, hoping the storms the meteorologist had promised would hold off until after the wedding. With the guests gone and nothing on the books for the following two days, the sky could open up for all she cared.

"Stella James, this place is impressive." Liam's voice was full of wonder as they reached the last room on the second floor.

Wonder that was making her heart beat a little too fast.

She ignored the butterflies tumbling at the sound of her full name on his lips. "Thanks. Watching it grow has been worth all the struggle. Of course, I guess you of all people can understand that. You've grown quite your own little empire in Colorado." She winced at the admission that she'd kept up with his life.

An odd twitch of emotion crossed his face before he quickly replaced it with one of his dazzling smiles. "Would you mind showing me the boat house?"

A soft flicker of light lit up the hall window as the storm drew closer. "If we hurry, I think we can beat the rain."

Whatever storm was blowing in from the west couldn't be half as bad as the storm brewing in her chest. For twelve years, she'd harbored some serious resentment for the man standing beside her, but now that he was here in the flesh all she could focus on was his lean body, and heavenly scent.

Back down the steps and out through the French doors, Stella weaved her way through the garden toward the boat house as the first few sprinkles fell. The clear skies blanketed in stars had quickly been replaced by an inky, endless black. Just as her bare feet landed on the top board of the three small steps leading down to the boat house, large drops began to thud against the dock.

Between the dark, and the slight tilt of her world, it took several tries before she managed to get the key into the lock and open the door. Holding the door open, she ushered Liam in as the flood gates opened up.

"Well, that escalated quickly," Liam called over his shoulder.

With only the porch light streaming in through the front window, Stella watched as he crossed the darkened room to the far window, and stared out over the open water. There was something far more alluring about watching him move in the shadows.

Stepping in next to him, Stella glanced out the window, amazed by the sight. Bathed in the soft porch light, the fat raindrops were hitting so rapidly it looked like the lake was boiling.

"I don't know about you, but I think I'll wait for the heavy rain to pass before I trek back across the lawn." Her voice came out huskier than she intended.

"Afraid you might melt?" Liam teased.

Stella shot him a sarcastic smile. "Or worse, end up soaking wet."

"Getting a little wet is not always a bad thing."

Before she could save herself, a bright flash of lightning split across the sky. The sudden burst of electricity charged the air around them. In an instant, Stella found herself right where they'd left off twelve years earlier.

Throwing caution into the raging storm, she lifted her hands around his neck, and pulled him home.

Chapter Three

Stella was vaguely aware of her cell phone ringing somewhere in the distance. Her eyes were too heavy, her mouth too dry, and based on the pounding against her skull, it was going to take three days to recover from the hangover. Why in the hell had she drunk so much wine?

And then she heard it.

The soft snore coming from beside her.

Stella's eyes flashed open as the memories of the night before assaulted her mind. The storm blowing in from the west. The magnificent man standing in her boat house. The large amount of wine she'd consumed to drown out his memory.

What had she done?

Easing off the bed, she grabbed her rumpled dress from the floor, and spotted her cell phone on the table by the door next to an empty bottle of Merlot. She was never drinking again.

Ever.

With her cell phone in hand, she tiptoed across the floor to the bathroom and locked the door behind her. Her reflection in the mirror looked as bad as she felt, but that was the least of her concerns at the moment. Right now, the only thing she needed to concentrate on was getting dressed, and making her escape before the sleeping beast woke up.

Untangling the mess of black fabric, she tried to quietly stuff herself back into the form-fitting dress. A task that would have been easier if not for the wine induced fog covering her brain, and the panic pressing on her chest. She was panting like she'd run a half marathon.

Just as she reached for the door handle, her cell phone once again rang.

Swiping the screen, she pressed the phone to her ear, cupping her free hand around the base, and spoke softly. "Hey, sweetie."

"Grandma's making pancakes before church." Her daughter's sweet voice trilled through the phone. "She said I should call and let you know since you weren't here. Where are you anyway?"

How had she been so careless? "I'm really sorry about that, sweet girl. I was so tired after the wedding and clean up that I must've accidently fallen asleep in my office."

Stella hated lying to her daughter. Not that she didn't tell little white lies all the time. The kind of lies all parents told their kids when they didn't have the answers to eight-million trivial questions a day, but this lie felt wrong.

Or maybe it was the fact that she'd slept with the enemy that felt so wrong.

"Why are you whispering?" Willa never missed a thing.

Ninety-nine percent of the time, Stella loved her daughter's perceptiveness. Willa was a smart girl, far brighter than most the kids her age, but this was one time Stella could have done without all the brains.

"Your call woke me up, so my voice hasn't woken up yet. Happens when you get old like me." She felt the lies piling up.

"Mom, you're thirty-five. You're not *that* old yet." She wasn't sure if the emphasis on *that* was supposed to make her feel better or worse, but right now the only thing Stella felt was nauseated. Between the hangover and the lies she was telling her own flesh and blood, her stomach was twisted into knots. "Well, you better hurry before I eat all the pancakes, or else you'll be stuck with the gross oatmeal because we ran out of cereal."

Stella felt a weak smile spread across her face. For as smart as Willa was, she was still only eight years old, and had the attention span to suit. "I'll be there as quick as I can."

"Okay. Love you, Momma."

"Love you more, Sweetie."

Stella took one last look at herself in the mirror, and wiped the black smudges from beneath her eyes. It had been almost nine years since she'd had to make the walk of shame after a one-night stand. Eight and half months later, she'd given birth to Willa.

Sure, she'd dated some over the years, but between the non-traditional relationship with Willa's dad, the business, and raising a daughter, dating had taken a backseat in life. What had made the priority list, however, was always coming home to sleep in her own bed on the rare occasion that she found a male companion to spend some time with.

Slowly turning the knob, Stella held her breath as she slipped out of the bathroom door, and locked eyes with Liam.

Good thing she was already holding her breath because the sight of him sitting on the edge of the bed would have stolen it away. His pants were already on, but the muscles peeking out from the half-buttoned shirt were bringing back memories that caused her skin to heat.

"Hi." She pushed the word out past the lump in her throat.

"I thought maybe you had left already." Liam broke eye contact, and went about dressing himself.

Was he mad?

The calm, cool, collected Liam from last night was gone, replaced by a man with a chip on his shoulder. The shift threw Stella for a loop. Was he mad because he thought she'd snuck out? Or was he mad because she hadn't left, and now he had to face her in the light of day?

"Liam, I…" Not wanting to bring Willa into her mess, Stella searched for the right words.

"Made a mistake. I know." Liam's gruff voice filled in her silence.

Mistake wasn't quite the word she was thinking but based on the waves of annoyance rolling off him, maybe it was more fitting. "I was going to say I needed to head out, but I'm glad we're on the same page." Her defensiveness reared its ugly head.

"I'm sure you are." Liam bent down to grab his dress shoes.

Okay, so getting drunk and sleeping with her ex hadn't exactly been on her bucket list either, but what the hell was his problem? He didn't seem to have a problem with the idea last night. "What the hell is that supposed to mean?"

"Nothing…*Sweetie.*"

Stella let out a ragged breath. He'd heard her conversation.

For half a second, she thought about correcting the misunderstanding. How no man was at home waiting for her arrival. No man in her bed, missing her warmth next to him last night. It was just her and Willa.

He's leaving. The thought sobered her.

She didn't owe Liam Scott a thing, much less an explanation for her private phone calls. He would leave, like he had twelve years ago. And like then, he wouldn't be looking back. So, what if he thought she had cheated on some non-existent man? She'd given up caring what he thought a long time ago.

Liam Scott could think whatever he wanted about her, as long as he did it halfway across the continental US.

Crossing the small room, Stella opened the exterior door. "I assume you can find your way across the lawn."

*****

Liam cringed as the cold, wet earth squished between his toes. The rain from the previous night's storm had pushed out any semblance of warmth from the mid-April day. As he moved up the lawn, a chill ran across his skin, making him wish he had ignored Stella's curt invitation to leave, and finished dressing. At the very least, he should have put on his shoes.

It wasn't the first time he'd been escorted to the door, but it was the first time he'd been kicked out half-dressed and barefoot.

But it seemed *firsts* were the order of the day.

It was the first time he'd ever slept with an ex. First time he'd wanted to both kiss and kill said ex at the same time. And definitely the first time he'd been a co-conspirator in an affair—well, that he knew of anyway—though he had plausible deniability on that front.

The thing was, he'd been shocked to see Stella wasn't wearing a ring. A certain finger on her left hand had been the first thing he'd checked out. And the moment he saw it was bare, he'd moved on to more entertaining parts.

Now, as he trudged across the soggy grass, he felt like a schmuck.

Deniability aside, the last thing Liam wanted was to show up after all these years, and mess up Stella's life. Of course, the Stella he used to know would have never cheated. She was sweet and innocent. A pure heart made of gold.

But twelve years was a long time, and people changed.

Hell, he'd certainly changed. He was far from the scared boy he'd been at twenty-three. That version of himself had been afraid of the future, unsure of where it was leading him. He'd been terrified of tying his roots into knots so young. Instead of a ring around his finger, it'd felt like a noose around his neck.

When Liam had asked Stella to marry him, he'd made a poor assumption that they would wait to get married. She'd been dropping so many hints he felt like he didn't have a choice but to get down on one knee or risk losing her. The ring was supposed to be a placeholder of sorts. A symbol of his eventual intentions. He knew he wasn't ready to make that kind of commitment, but he needed to buy some time.

In the end, it hadn't mattered. He'd lost her all the same.

Liam's thoughts drifted back to that last morning with Stella. She'd been wearing one of his old, faded t-shirts. Her hair piled into a mess on top of her head. And the same as this morning, her day-old makeup had left black smudges beneath her lashes. He hadn't cared though. She was beautiful all the same.

Slipping into his truck, he closed his eyes. He could still see her sitting at their small dining room table in their second-floor apartment. The devastation pooling in her eyes. An image that was permanently burned into his brain.

Stella had been pushing for him to choose a wedding date, but there was another conversation he needed to have first. A conversation he knew wasn't going to go over well, but before he could broach the subject, she'd gone through his email, and found the letter confirming his start date for a new job.

In Colorado.

How many years would it take for him to forget the awful things they'd said to each other after that? Reason had left in a hurry, leaving chaos to reign over the fight that ensued. They'd both said some pretty horrible things. Things he was certain neither one of them meant.

All he'd wanted was to go out and live. Experience the world. He'd lived his entire life in South Carolina. He wanted to explore, feel something different before settling down and having kids. As much as they talked about traveling, he knew once they were married, she'd want a family, and starting a family meant their plans would turn into dreams that never came to fruition.

He'd needed to go while he still could.

In hindsight, he knew he had gone about things the wrong way, but that was the thing about the past, it was easier to see your mistakes after you royally fucked up.

He'd never intended for them to break up. Sure, he'd been young and dumb, but he naively thought she would come with him. At the very least, they'd stay together, and visit one another as often as they could.

It wasn't a foolproof plan, but it was the best he had. Right up until the moment she'd been snooping through his email. Maybe it was the fact that he was actually hiding something, but the violation of privacy had hit him in the gut. Before he could get a handle on his anger, Stella had railroaded him with false accusations of not wanting to be with her at all. It was like throwing fuel on a fire.

Backed so far in the corner he couldn't breathe, Liam's anger had exploded. In a rush of emotion, he'd let the damming words fly from lips. Words he never meant, and would come to regret. Words that put an end to any future they had.

I never wanted to propose but you gave me no choice.

Starting his truck, Liam pulled onto the highway, and headed back to Carefree as the memories swirled.

It struck him then, the parallel between that last day with Stella, and the past twenty-four hours. Irony had grown a sense of humor. Making love in a storm only for him to walk away the next morning with his tail tucked between his legs. Two people wanting two different things. It was like the past twelve years had paused, and they'd somehow picked up right where they'd left off.

The only difference, this time he wasn't leaving town.

Twenty minutes later, Liam pulled into the driveway he shared with his sister and brother-in-law. Renting the studio apartment above Kat's detached garage had seemed like a great idea when he'd first come back to Carefree, but now that she was staring at him from the gravel, watching his walk of shame, maybe he needed to reconsider living next to one of his nosy siblings.

"Looks like you found more than your cell phone last night." Kat raised a brow as he stepped out of the truck.

Before he could tell her to buzz off, she clutched the hood of her car, and doubled over in pain.

"Kat!" Liam ran to his sister's side. "What's wrong? Where's Brooks?"

"Right behind you," Brooks called as he rushed down the steps, a duffle bag slung over his shoulder. His face a few shades whiter than normal.

Liam's chest tightened. "The baby's coming? Isn't it too early?"

"She's been having contractions all morning. I told her not to overdo it last night. Not that she listens to anyone." Brooks threw the bag in the back seat and came back to where Kat was leaning on the hood.

"I'm right here, you know. I can hear you." Kat pushed herself back into a standing position. "Technically, thirty-seven weeks is considered full term. So, Stella, huh?"

Liam scrubbed a hand through his hair. "What the hell, Kat. We're not talking about this now. You need to get to the hospital because I'm not delivering my niece, and Brooks looks like he could pass out any minute."

"Oh, you two calm the hell down. My contractions are five minutes apart, which means I have roughly three minutes for you to tell me why you're just now showing up, still wearing the same tux from last night. Well, half of it anyway." Kat's eyes slid down to his bare feet.

"It's not a story worth telling. Nothing's going to come of it so you can put away your cupid wings. She's off the market."

"What do you mean *off the market*?" Kat gave him a curious look.

"What do you think I mean, she's with someone." He was not in the mood for Kat's favorite game of twenty questions. Gently grabbing Kat's arm, he tried to usher her to the passenger side. "Come on, get in the car."

"I don't know what you heard, but you've been misinformed. I already checked." Kat shot him a sly smile.

Liam opened the passenger door. "Your skills are getting weak then, because someone was calling this morning to see why she didn't come home last night."

What would Kat know anyway? Sure, the diner was the source of most the gossip in Carefree, but Stella didn't live in Carefree. On second thought, he didn't know where Stella lived, but considering her business was almost in Pebble Creek, he would imagine that's where she spent her time.

"Are you sure that wasn't just her—" Kat's words drifted as she bent over in pain.

"Her what?" Shit, now he needed to know what Kat knew.

"Oh look, time…for me…to go," Kat sputtered the words out between grunts of pain.

Closing the door, Liam watched the car back out of the drive, and head down the road as Kat's words echoed in his head. What the hell had she been trying to say?

He thought back to the conversation he'd overheard this morning. Stella's voice had been low and muffled by the door between them, but he'd made out some of the words.

"I'm sorry...I must have fallen asleep in my office...I'll be there as quick as I can...Love you more, sweetie."

She'd apologized and lied about where she was. She'd said *love you more* for God's sake. Who else would she say those things to other than a boyfriend or husband? He could see a roommate calling if she didn't come home, but you didn't tell your roommate you loved them more.

Whatever Kat thought she knew, she was wrong.

Stella James was off the market.

Chapter Four

One of the hardest lessons Stella had learned in life was not to dwell on things she couldn't change. It was wasted energy with no possibility of resolution.

It was one of the few lessons she could credit her father for teaching her. Only, she'd learned it in his absence. The man was a walking sack of empty promises.

Just like Liam.

The only difference between her father and her ex was Liam hadn't waited until they were married with a child to accuse her of trapping him into a marriage he never wanted. At least, he'd had the decency to run out on her before they walked down the aisle. Her father, however, had waited until the eve of her tenth birthday before he'd walked out and never looked back.

It had been late the night before her birthday, and she couldn't sleep for the excitement of turning ten, when she heard the voices coming through her bedroom wall. It wasn't unusual to hear her parents fight, but this time felt different. The following morning, her father hadn't been at the breakfast table. When she questioned where he was, her mother had simply said he needed some air.

That had been twenty-five years ago.

In the quiet of her office, Stella pushed the old memories back in their dark hole, and stared at the box of centerpieces sitting in the corner. She'd spent the better part of the past four days obsessing over the stupid thing but it was time to close that chapter of her life.

No, this wasn't a chapter. It was a tangent in her story. A pothole in the road.

Liam undoubtably was back in Colorado by now, so there was no reason for the box to remain in her office any longer. She needed to drop it off at Kat's diner and be done with the Scott family once and for all.

Stella walked over to the box and bent to pick it up as Whitney stopped in the doorway. "You finally taking those back?"

"Yeah, I'm going to pick Willa up from school and drive into Carefree. I need to be done with this."

Whitney shot her a questioning glance. "You need to be done with the box sitting in here or with the man that was supposed to take them when he left Saturday night?"

Stella hesitated. Though her relationship with Whitney had evolved from employee-employer to best friends years ago, there were still some things she wasn't ready to admit to. Like sleeping with the

Devil for one. "I told you, I gave him a tour and then he left in a hurry before the storm started."

Why was it every time Liam came up, nothing but lies left her mouth?

"Uh huh, I'm sure you gave him a tour alright. A tour of Stellaland."

A blush flourished across her cheeks. "Would you stop before someone hears you?"

"Admit that I'm right and I'll stop."

Ignoring Whitney's banter, Stella brushed by her best friend. "I'm going to the school now. If you need anything, call me."

"It was that good, huh?" Whitney followed Stella as she headed for the front door.

God, if Whitney only knew. It was the most amazing night she'd had in...forever.

Maybe it was the wine and nostalgia, but Liam had awakened a part of her she hadn't known she was missing. Like a powerful earthquake, she'd felt the aftershocks for two days. A tingling sensation rippled across her skin just thinking about it.

Not that it mattered. Her little side trip down memory lane was over. Nothing but hurt and heartbreak was at the end of that road.

Reaching the front door, Stella turned back to face her friend. "Did you confirm the bounce house for Willa's party?"

"Way to change the subject, but yeah, I did. They'll be at the house at eleven Saturday morning."

"Perfect. Thanks, Whit. I don't know what I would do without you."

"Crumble into a hot mess?" Whitney smiled. "Hey, is Ranger Rick coming to the party?"

"You have to stop calling him that before you accidentally say it in front of him." Stella smiled at the nickname Whitney had given Willa's dad. "And yes, he's supposed to be back in time for the party."

Walking out to her car, Stella placed the box in the backseat and closed the door. As she drove toward Willa's school, she made a mental checklist of all the things she needed to do for her daughter's party. For one, she needed to call and make sure Rick knew what time things were starting.

Rick Goldstein was a kind and decent person, albeit the most boring person Stella had ever met. Extremely intelligent, he was also the kind of man who followed all the rules and played it safe. Thus, Whitney's nickname of Ranger Rick. He was like an overgrown safety patrol.

Stella supposed they were all great qualities for his profession as a nuclear engineer, but it didn't exactly make for an entertaining partner, which is why she'd never been interested in having a real relationship with him. She would never deny him access to Willa, and quite honestly, he was amazing with their daughter, but Stella wasn't interested in tying her life to him any more than she already had. They'd learned how to co-parent without being an item years ago and it was working fine.

Of course, that hadn't stopped Stella from hooking up with him from time to time.

Rick wasn't the most passionate man, but they had a common connection, and she'd made it abundantly clear to him that they would never be more than two friends who occasionally shared a bed. Rick was her safe zone. A means to an end. And he'd been good with it.

Friends with benefits was the only time she'd seen him do something borderline risky, but he was a man after all. When presented with sex, what man said no?

They'd always been careful to keep that part of their friendship private to not confuse Willa. The last thing she wanted to do was give their daughter false hope for something that would never be.

Pulling up to the metal awning of Pebble Creek Elementary, Stella waited for the teacher to open the door, and Willa to climb in the backseat. "Hey kiddo. How was your day?"

Willa grabbed her seatbelt and clicked it into place. "It was good. Mrs. Rose tried to give me some hard problems during my pullout time, but I figured them out. She also said I might be able to enter the science fair if I wanted to. It's normally just for fifth grade, but she said if I brought her a proposal, she would have Principal Moore review it."

"That's awesome." Stella's heart smiled.

She'd known from early on that Willa was ahead of the curve, but Stella hadn't known how smart her daughter was until she'd placed her into a Pre-K program. The program's director said she'd never seen anything like it. The director had then reached out to the school and recommended that Willa be placed into kindergarten early. There had been push back because of her age, but once they conceded to an evaluation, they'd been just as impressed.

Stella had to attribute Willa's intelligence to her father's genetics. She was decently smart, but nothing like the two of them.

The thing Stella loved most about the school was how they'd handled Willa. In efforts to give her a normal school experience, they'd kept her with kids her age, but every day when the kids in her class did their small group reading, Willa would visit a classroom one grade higher to do more advanced work.

This year, however, she was leaving her third-grade classroom to visit Mrs. Rose's fifth grade class.

The thought of her eight-year-old being mixed in with ten and eleven-year-olds had made Stella nervous, but the kids had accepted Willa happily.

"Why are we going this way?" Willa leaned her head toward the center of the car to better see out of the front window.

"We have to run an errand in Carefree. I thought maybe we could get milkshakes while we're in town. What do you think?"

"Milkshakes on a Wednesday? I think you're the best mom ever." A bright smile spread across Willa's face.

Stella let out a soft chuckle. "You don't have to butter me up, I'm already getting you a treat."

"Did you know that 'butter me up' comes from ancient India? They would throw butter at the statues of their gods to seek favor and forgiveness."

Stella glanced in the rearview mirror. "How do you know that?" The expanse of her daughter's knowledge never ceased to amaze her.

Willa shrugged as she stared out the side window. "I learned it on the History Channel."

*****

Liam was losing his damn mind. If he'd known he would be sweating bullets while covered in some seriously gross food smears, he never would have agreed to help out at the diner while Kat was busy being a new mom.

How in the hell did she make this look so easy?

He'd spent plenty of time sitting at the counter and never once did she look as disheveled as he felt. And she'd been eight months pregnant. Eight years running an outdoor adventure company was nothing compared to trying to run a diner.

"I'm going to have to charge you for the amount of food you're wearing on your shirt."

Liam turned to find José, Kat's business partner, staring him down. "Seriously, how does she make this look so easy?"

José let out a soft chuckle. "Your sister's a rock star. You remind me of her when I first came to work here. She was a mess back then."

The thought of Kat struggling in the beginning gave Liam a little comfort. "Well, maybe there is hope for me."

"No offense, man, but I'm not holding my breath."

"Thanks."

Liam was thankful the lunch rush was over. The diner was mostly empty at the moment and should stay that way until the dinner crowd picked up. At the sound of the bell above the door, he turned in time to see his past come waltzing in with a young girl trailing behind her.

After the way their last interaction ended, he was surprised to see Stella. And based on the look on her face, the feeling was mutual.

"What are you doing here?" Stella gave him a once over before setting the box he'd forgotten on the counter.

"I'm helping out around here while Kat's taking maternity leave." Liam wiped a hand across his shirt and wished he didn't look like a kid after a food fight. Not that it mattered what Stella thought of him, but he would have preferred to look a little more presentable and less like a joke.

"That's sweet of you." A brief smile crossed Stella's lips before quickly fading. "Shouldn't you be back in Colorado by now.

"I came back." Out of the corner of his eye, he saw José retreat to the kitchen.

"You flew home and then came back because your sister had a baby?"

"No, I moved back a few weeks ago." He watched Stella's eyes widen like she'd seen a ghost.

"What about your company?" Her voice jumped up an octave.

Liam grabbed a rag and wiped the countertop, avoiding eye contact. "I sold it. Can I get you two anything while you're here?"

He had to assume the young girl standing next to her was Stella's daughter. There was an uncanny resemblance between the two.

Without a question, the girl took a seat at the bar. "What kind of milkshakes do you have?"

"Willa, I don't know if they serve milkshakes here. We can get one somewhere else."

Liam stood up taller and flashed a bright smile at the girl. "We have the best milkshakes in town."

What are you doing?

Their last conversation hadn't ended well and here he was inviting Stella and her presumed daughter to sit down and stay a while. No wonder someone had been calling her to see why she hadn't come home from the wedding. Not only did she have a man waiting on her, but a daughter too. This was not a situation he needed to be in the middle of.

Unfortunately, his head didn't agree. Call it morbid curiosity, but something deep inside of him wanted Stella to stay. Even if only for a few minutes.

"Do you have an Oreo milkshake? That's my favorite, but I can settle for chocolate." The young girl interrupted his wayward thoughts.

"Of course. One Oreo milkshake coming up…if it's okay with your mom?" Liam glanced at Stella, waiting for her to confirm or deny the girl was hers.

"It's fine."

So, he was right. Stella James had a daughter. It made sense, she was a beautiful woman, but damn, Stella James had a daughter. "And a strawberry milkshake with whipped cream for you? With a strawberry instead of a cherry on top, of course."

Stella shot him a hard stare but nodded. "Sure."

Her daughter perked up. "How do you know what kind of milkshake my mom likes?"

"Lucky guess." Liam shrugged. Shit, he hadn't thought that through. Her daughter was perceptive.

"No, it wasn't a guess." The girl eyed him. "Statistically, you would guess vanilla because most adults like it better than chocolate, but you also knew she wanted a strawberry and not a cherry."

What the hell? He was getting schooled on milkshake preferences by a little kid. Liam glanced at Stella for help.

"Willa James, don't be rude. Liam and I were old friends. We may have had a milkshake or two in our day."

Willa extended her hand toward him and smiled. "Well, it's nice to meet you, old friend Liam."

Liam couldn't help his laugh. This kid was something. "Nice to meet you, too, new friend Willa."

Willa James. She had Stella's last name. Stella still wasn't wearing a ring. So many questions ran through his mind. Was Willa's father still in the picture? Was someone else playing stepdad? Shaking off the thoughts, Liam took a step back from the counter.

He didn't need to worry about who was waiting at home for them. "Two shakes coming up."

Scribbling on the order pad, he handed the ticket off to Wendy, one of the regular waitresses. The only thing José had taught him was how to run the register and where to put the dirty dishes. As for the rest, the wait staff could handle that.

"So old friend Liam, you used to live in Colorado?"

"Willa, we don't pry in people's lives." Stella ran her hand down her daughter's hair before glancing back at Liam. "I'm sorry."

"No, it's okay. I don't mind." For all the tension he felt between him and Stella, not an ounce of that was directed at the kid. He turned his attention back to Willa. "I did. I lived in Denver for a few years, and then I moved to Dillon."

Willa studied him for a second before finally responding. "I've never heard of Dillon."

"Have you heard of Vail or Breckenridge?"

"Yes, those are the popular ski resorts. There's Aspen and Keystone resorts, too. Did you know there's a place called Purgatory Ski Resort? It's not near Breckenridge, but I'm not sure why anyone would want to ski at a place called Purgatory."

"I'm impressed. Dillon is pretty close to Keystone. So, you must like to ski?" Everyone and their grandmother knew the names Vail and Breckenridge, but Keystone wasn't a widely talked about resort outside of the Rockies.

"I've never been skiing before, but I like the Discovery Channel."

Just then, Stella's purse began to ring. Liam watched as she pulled out her phone and a slight frown creased her lips.

"Sorry, I need to take this. It's the office." Turning to her daughter, Stella spoke softly, "Stay right here. Your milkshake should be out in a second."

50

"I'll keep an eye on her," Liam added like he was some sort of babysitter.

A moment later, Wendy appeared with the milkshakes.

"So, Liam who used to live in Colorado, you didn't work in a diner in Dillon did you?"

He wasn't sure if it was more of a statement or a question, but she was looking at him like she was waiting for a response. "No, I actually owned an expedition company. This diner belongs to my sister, but she just had a baby, so I'm helping out."

"Is it a girl or boy?"

Liam smiled with pride. "A little girl. Her name is Penelope."

"That's a cute name." Willa drank some of her milkshake before looking back up at him. "So, you took groups of people out on adventures?"

"Basically, yeah. We did a lot of skiing in the winter, but in the summer, we did stuff like rafting."

"That's kind of what Jackson does, but we don't really have snow in the winter. It would be cool if we had more snow, but it never does."

Liam felt a pang in his gut at the mention of another man. "Is Jackson your dad?"

"No, Jackson works for my mom. He does trips for the groups that come and stay."

"So, he's not your mom's boyfriend?"

Willa studied him for a moment. "Why do you want to know if my mom has a boyfriend?"

The question took Liam by surprise. "Just making conversation." He shrugged.

"How about a deal, Liam from Dillon. You give me two math problems. If I get them right, you tell me why you want to know if my mom has a boyfriend. And if I get them wrong, I'll tell you if she does or not."

He couldn't believe this kid. She definitely had Stella's sass. "Okay, deal."

Liam thought for a second. She was obviously a smart kid with some serious perception skills, but she had to be less than ten years old. He tried to remember what kind of math he would have done at her age. Was she into multiplication yet?

"Alright smarty pants, what's seven times six?"

"Forty-two." She spouted the answer a half a second after he'd gotten the words out. "I'll give you that one for free."

"Fine, what's twenty-four times fifteen?" Liam threw out the first two-digit numbers he thought of.

It took her a few seconds longer this time, but Willa smiled up at him and said, "Three-hundred and sixty. Final question."

Jeez, who was this kid? He couldn't have done that one in his head if he tried. Liam felt his competitive nature take hold. "Final problem, what's the square root of one-hundred and sixty-nine?"

Willa cocked her tiny head and smiled. "Sixteen minus seven, plus four...or I guess I could've said thirteen. My turn. Why do you want to know if my mom has a boyfriend?"

Chapter Five

Stella glanced at the name displayed across her phone's screen and sighed. She had a bad feeling Whitney wasn't calling because she was being nosy, and the last thing Stella needed was another problem on her plate. Standing in a room with her ex, who had apparently decided to move home, was all she could handle at the moment.

Stepping away from the counter, Stella moved toward the door, out of ear shot. "Hey Whit, what's up?"

"I hate to be the bearer of bad news, but we have a tiny problem. I got a call from Jackson. He's in the ER with a broken leg."

Stress coiled in Stella's shoulders. "Whit, that's not a tiny problem. He's supposed to be leading The Stanley Group on a paddle down Battery Creek Saturday."

"I know. We'll figure it out. I'll make some calls and see what our options are."

The tension in her shoulders worked its way up the base of Stella's skull. She was supposed to be focusing on Willa's party and now she needed to find someone who knew their way through the marsh, and wouldn't get The Stanley Group lost.

Battery Creek was a network of waterways that splintered through the marsh. It was easy to get turned around in the tall grasses or get hung up on shallow sands. Jackson had grown up in the area and knew the waterway like the back of his hand, but there was no way he would be able to paddle his way through with a broken leg.

Turning back toward the counter, her eyes locked on Willa and Liam. The two looked like they were in some sort of deep conversation. "Oh, no."

"What's going on?" Whitney's voice perked up at the hint of Stella's unease.

"Nothing, I just need to take care of something. Start making some calls. I have to go for now."

She hit end and worked her way back to the counter. "What are you two discussing?" Stella glanced between the two people she'd never intended to meet. Whatever they were discussing looked intense...at least on Liam's part.

Liam scrubbed a hand through his hair, and she tried her best to ignore how attractive his bed head made him look. "I'm fairly certain I got hustled by your kid."

Stella let out a sigh. "Did she make you give her math problems?"

His eyes shifted to Willa and then back to her. She'd seen the look before. He was trying to decide how much trouble he was about to get her daughter into. "It was a couple of questions. No big deal."

There was more to the story. Stella sensed it in his hesitation. "What was the deal?"

"Deal? There was no deal." Liam's eyes didn't quite connect with hers.

"She's onto you. You should really work on your poker face." Willa chimed in between slurps.

The pain that was building bloomed into a full-on headache. "Wil, we've talked about this. It's not polite to trick strangers."

"He's not a stranger. He's your old friend, who knows what kind of milkshake you like, which is melting by the way."

"Semantics, Willa James. You know what I mean. He's a stranger to you."

"Fine." Willa slid her empty glass toward Liam and looked up at him. "I'm sorry I tricked you, Liam. My mom doesn't have a boyfriend."

"Willa!" A heated blush raced up her neck, and across her cheeks.

Willa smiled up at her. "What? If I lost, I was supposed to tell him if you had a boyfriend or not."

Stella took a deep breath to regain her composure. She would drill her daughter on the exact conversation when they got in the car, but right now she didn't have time to focus on why her ex wanted to know if she had a boyfriend. Jackson was out of commission, likely for the summer, and she had to figure out a plan B.

"Come on, we need to head back. I've gotta find a replacement for Jackson by Saturday."

"What's wrong with Jackson?" Liam and Willa questioned her at the same time.

"Jinx, you owe me a soda." Willa laughed.

Stella understood why her daughter would ask, but Liam didn't know her employee from Adam. "He's at the ER with a broken leg." Stella turned her attention to Liam. "Do you know him?"

"No, Willa mentioned he worked for you."

"You two fit a lot of conversation into a short amount of time."

"Mom! Liam owned an expedition company in Colorado. He can fill in for Jackson. He'd be perfect."

Sweat broke out above her brow. How did she explain to her eight-year-old there was no way in hell she was letting Liam Scott anywhere near her business? The man had caused enough damage to last her a lifetime. No way was she about to bring him into the fold. Even if she was desperate.

Even if hell froze over.

"Willa, Liam is already helping out his sister here. I'm sure he's really busy. Come on, we need to head back."

"I really don't mind," Liam interjected.

"See, Mom."

"No!" The word came out hard and fast. The whole world was out to ruin her day. First Jackson, now Liam and Willa. She had to end this now. Locking eyes with Liam, Stella lowered her voice. "Can I speak to you alone for a moment?"

Stella walked to the end of the counter where it opened up into the diner. She felt Liam's presence before she turned around to face him. "Listen, I don't know what this is, but I don't need you stepping in trying to save the day, okay. I'm fine. I can take care of my business."

"I didn't mean to imply you couldn't, I just happen to have a lot of free time on my hands. I thought I would help an old friend."

"No. We're not friends. That ship sailed a long time ago. And I would appreciate it if you weren't going around asking my eight-year-old about my personal life."

"Stel, I didn't—"

"You were right, the other night was a mistake." Stella interrupted him before he could finish his thought. She didn't want to know what he did or didn't plan to say. "I had too much wine, and I stupidly thought you would be gone by the next day. End of story. You chose to ditch me a long time ago, and I would prefer if you stuck to that plan."

"Ditch you? I didn't ditch you." The easy-going Liam was gone. "You told me to go and not look back."

Angry laughter bubbled up from her chest. "I'm not doing this with you right now."

"Right, because when you don't want to do something that's perfectly fine. But when I'm not ready to do something, I'm the damn Devil."

"Grow up, Liam."

"For the record." Liam stepped in closer. "I did grow up. I've changed a lot over the years. I'm not the same scared boy I used to be, but I see I'm not the only one who's changed. The milkshakes are on the house."

Before she could utter another word, Liam turned away, and headed into the kitchen.

Dammit, why did she let him get under her skin that way? It had been twelve years. Whatever they may or may not have had in the past was ancient history. Walking back over to her daughter, Stella grabbed a twenty from her wallet, and threw it on the counter. She wouldn't owe him anything.

"Come on, sweetie. Let's go."

*****

Twelve years, and she was still putting all the blame on him. Liam wasn't sure why he expected anything more. She hadn't owned up to her part in the disaster back then, why the hell would she take responsibility now?

The last thing he had wanted was to confront their past in the middle of the diner, and in front of her kid. He was simply trying to offer her an olive branch, and she'd looked at him like a snake with two heads.

Fine. If Stella James didn't want his help, it was no skin off his back.

"Dammit." Liam pushed his way into the kitchen. "Why do women have to be so damn stubborn?"

"I hope that's a rhetorical question." José looked up from where he was cleaning the grill. "Because I don't have an answer for you."

"You know, you try to extend an olive branch, and they break it in half like it's some useless twig. It's so damn frustrating. Women are so frustrating, José. Sexy and frustrating. And you know what the crazy thing is?"

José shot him a grin. "No, but I bet you're going to tell me."

"I'm not the only one to blame. I wanted us to be together, but because I wasn't ready to walk down the damn aisle at that very moment, I'm the bad guy." Liam paced around the kitchen. His head ready to explode. "She's the one that went through my email and then wouldn't let me explain. For once, you would think she could admit that part of it was her fault. But noooo. Heaven forbid, she take any responsibility. I mean seriously, is it that damn hard to say, *Hey Liam, I made mistakes, too. I said and did I didn't mean.*"

"I'm going to assume that's rhetorical also?"

Liam ignored José's remarks and continued his rant while he paced around the room. "I was trying to be nice last weekend. Take an interest in her business. See how things were going in her life and you know what I got? Jumped. She jumped me. And what was I supposed to do? It was late, we were drunk, and she looked amazing in that skintight, black, come-get-me dress. Was I supposed to tell her no? I mean, who tells a fine-ass woman, who's climbing up your body, no. But it turns out, she only wanted me because she thought I was leaving. What the hell is that?"

José laughed. "First world problems?"

He wasn't wrong. The world had bigger issues than who was to blame for a breakup twelve years ago, but for the past four days, Stella was all Liam could think about. He felt like a damn fool lost in the desert. She'd given him a tiny sip of life Saturday night and now he was thirsting for more.

Of course, things could have gone smoother given she'd shown up like a mirage in the diner, but for as sexy as Stella James was, she was as equally frustrating.

At least he had gained one valuable piece of information. Stella was single. He'd completely misunderstood the phone call Sunday morning. She hadn't cheated on a husband or boyfriend after all. It had been her daughter calling to see where she was.

Images of Stella's naked body pressed against his swirled in his mind.

Things may not have worked out before, but there was no denying the chemistry they shared in the bedroom. What had happened between them Saturday night was almost magical. They weren't the same young kids they'd been back then. They were grown-ass adults with different desires. He may not have known what he'd wanted in his early twenties, but Liam knew exactly what he wanted now.

He wanted Stella.

No rings. No promises of forever. Just their bodies pressed together.

She'd wanted it as much as he had. Hell, she'd made the first move. He'd seen the desire in her eyes, no matter how much she tried to claim it was a mistake.

Stella was right about one thing. He'd walked away before, but no job was calling him across the country this time. The only thing calling him now was a yearning to finish what they'd started Saturday night.

Liam stopped pacing and faced José. "Anything else you need me to help out with before I go?"

"No." The cook tossed the towel he was holding over his left shoulder. "I have a full staff for the evening."

"Great, because I could really use a beer right about now." A beer and some time to develop a plan. He was single, and so was Stella, so there was no reason why they couldn't be single together while enjoying a few adult activities. He just had to find a way to get her on board.

"Your sister keeps a bottle of Southern Comfort in the bottom desk drawer in the office." José shot him a grin.

"Why does that not surprise me?" Liam shook his head and laughed. "Maybe another time, right now there's a cooler and a boat calling my name."

Liam and José turned in unison at the sound of the kitchen door swinging open. Wendy appeared holding up a twenty. "This was on the counter. What should I do with it?"

Dammit. Stella had left money to cover the milkshakes, plus some.

She wasn't going to make this easy on him. He had a lot of ground to make up if he was going to get her in his bed, considering she wasn't even willing to accept a free milkshake.

Maybe this Jackson guy getting hurt was the opening he needed. He wasn't sure what all Pebble Creek had booked for the summer, but with a broken leg, the guy was likely out of commission for the next six to eight weeks. With any luck, it would give him six to eight weeks to live out some fantasies he'd had about his ex.

"Keep it." Liam gestured toward the bill Wendy was holding up. "I don't need the tip."

Wendy's mouth dropped open. "Are you sure?"

He wasn't about to explain his *first world problems*—as José had called them—to one of his sister's employees. "Yeah, I'm completely sure."

"Don't tell Kat, but you're way cooler than your sister." Wendy flashed him a sexy smile, and slowly slid the bill into her apron.

A genuine laugh rumbled through his chest. "I've always been way cooler than Kat."

Well, if things didn't work out like he hoped with Stella, there was always a Plan B.

Chapter Six

Stella dropped her head in her hands and let out a frustrated sigh. She and Whitney had been at it all day and had come up completely empty. She'd exhausted all of her contacts and not a single person could fill in for Jackson Saturday morning.

"How is this even possible?" Stella lifted her head, and glanced across the conference room table at Whitney. "We seriously have no one?"

"What if we let them do a self-guided tour?" Whitney asked.

"You can't be serious?" Stella looked her best friend dead in the eyes. "First of all, that's not the kind of service we offer. And second, how would they even get down there?"

"Whoa, I'm just throwing out ideas."

"I know." Stella scrubbed her hands up and down her face. "I'm just frustrated. I shouldn't take it out on you."

More than anything, she was frustrated there was a solution at her fingertips, but she couldn't let herself fall back into that trap. This was her business, her life, and the last time she'd trusted Liam with her life he'd ripped it into pieces. Just like her father, Liam had walked away and never looked back. And like with her father, she hadn't been enough for him to stay. He'd found some shiny new job in Colorado, and she'd been left to pick up the pieces by herself.

The business side of her knew she was out of options, and she needed his help, but the damaged woman inside her knew trusting a man only led to more trouble. It wasn't much, but this was her empire, and letting him in felt like a slippery slope.

"I know this isn't what you want to hear," Whitney spoke softly, "but I feel like we only have one other option."

It was like Whitney pulled the thought right out of her head. "I don't know if I can."

After they'd returned from the diner yesterday, Willa had happily told Whitney that Liam used to run his own excursion company and had offered to fill in. In her daughter's innocent eyes, it seemed like an easy fix. Stella had tried to push the notion to the side but without all the information, her daughter hadn't understood why Stella wouldn't want his help. She couldn't blame Willa for not understanding, but she also wasn't about to fill her eight-year-old in on her romantic past.

Stella's heart might be jaded for eternity, but Willa's heart was still pure, and Stella wanted to keep it that way as long as possible.

"Listen, I know you slept with the guy, but think of it like a business deal. No one's saying it has to be anything more."

"It's more than that." Stella hesitated, unable to say the words pressing on the back of her lips. She wanted to tell Whitney how he'd promised forever, and then ripped it out from under her feet. How he jabbed a knife so far into her heart that the scar would never heal. "He asked Willa if I had a boyfriend. What am I supposed to do with that?"

"Take it as a compliment. You're a hot momma. Maybe he has a mom fetish."

"Not helpful."

"Okay, listen James. We've exhausted all other avenues. We have a problem and a viable solution. It's time to decide what's more important, keeping up your business standards or cutting off your nose to spite your face."

"That's not fair," Stella protested, her temper beginning to boil.

"Hear me out. You won't have to be involved. I can handle everything. I'll meet him here Saturday morning to load up, while you get Willa's party set up. It will buy us some time to figure out a temporary replacement for Jackson."

Stella let the idea roll around her brain. Liam knew Battery Creek as well as anyone. Having a professional guide for The Stanley Group wouldn't be the worst thing. The firm was shelling out a lot of cash for their executive retreat, and if all went well there was potential for future bookings. Big spenders were exactly the kind of clients Stella needed.

For the sake of her business, she could do this.

It was just business. Nothing more.

"Okay." She really hoped this wasn't a big mistake.

"Okay." Whitney agreed. "Now all we need to do is figure out how to get in touch with him."

"Call his sister, Kat. She'll be able to get you in contact with him." Before Stella could continue, the front doorbell rang. "We don't have any appointments this afternoon, do we?"

"No, nothing's on the schedule." Whitney stood from her chair. "I'll go see who it is. I'm not expecting any deliveries today, but maybe it's the Prime fairy."

As Whitney left the room, Stella laid her head down on the conference table. The whole day had been one big ball of exhaustion, and all she'd done was make phone calls. Well, phone calls and wrestle with her past demons.

Normally, she'd go for a glass of wine to cool her rampant thoughts, but after the trouble her bottle of pinot had caused Saturday, wine was the last thing she wanted. She could, however, use a nice long soak in her clawfoot tub. If she were lucky, she could have Willa in bed by eight-thirty. Then, she could run a bath, and try to not fall asleep and drown.

"Hey Stella, someone's here to see you." Whitney's voice trailed in from behind her.

Stella didn't bother lifting her head. "Tell them I'm not here."

The one voice Stella never wanted to hear again drifted into the room. "Interesting, because it looks like you're sitting right there."

Closing her eyes, she said a quick prayer for the floor to open up and suck her in. When nothing happened, she took a deep breath and sat up, hoping red smudges weren't pressed into her face.

Spinning in her chair, Stella did her best to steady herself. Their plan had been for Whitney to handle everything, so why hadn't Whit told him she wasn't here. "Liam, we weren't expecting anyone. What are you doing here?"

"Well." Liam eased in the doorway. "I've come to ask for your help."

As if the emotional rollercoaster couldn't twist any more, now her ex was standing in her conference room asking her for help. How was she supposed to stay strong against his puppy-dog eyes?

*****

Liam knew it was a dangerous move crossing into enemy territory, but if there was any hope of Stella seeing how amazing their chemistry was together, he needed to devise a way to spend time with her. It was a risky move, but he also knew she had a weakness when it came to helping someone in need.

Stella would stand her stubborn ground to the ends of the earth not to accept support for herself, but she'd never been able to resist helping others. Now, he just had to convince her that's exactly what she'd be doing. Helping him and not the other way around.

He waited patiently as she took the bait. "And what is it you think I can help you with?"

This was going to be a delicate game of chess. He needed to make sure the focus stayed on how she would be saving his ass, not her own. No matter what the truth was. "Do you mind if I have a seat?"

Her eyes flickered to the chair next to her, and then back to him. "Sure, why not?"

"Thanks." Instead of crowding her space, Liam circled to the opposite side of the table and took a seat. He smiled to himself when she visibly relaxed. She was nervous with him this close. Good to note. "About six months ago, I found out my business partner was embezzling money from our company. As it turns out, he'd gotten himself pretty deep in a gambling hole and couldn't get out. It almost tanked our whole operation."

Stella raised a hand to her chest. "Liam, that's awful."

"Yeah, it pretty much sucked. Anyway, to make a long story short, I met with an investment firm who deals with companies similar to mine. I thought it would be the best way to save my ass, and my employees, but after a few months I realized my heart wasn't in it anymore. There was a lot of baggage, and with everything going on back here I decided to sell my options and walk away."

"I'm sure that wasn't an easy decision." Stella crossed her arms and rested them on the table.

"No, it wasn't. The thing is, I wanted to come home. I missed my family. Miles was getting married, Kat was pregnant, and I felt like I was missing out on so much. But now that I'm here..." Liam let the words drift, effectively pulling her right where he needed her.

—

68

"You don't know what to do with yourself." Stella finished his thought perfectly.

It wasn't entirely a lie. He had no idea what he was going to do with his life now, and he was losing his mind to boredom, but for the moment it was the ruse he needed.

"Exactly. I've been working six days a week for so long, I don't know what to do with all this free time. I suck at the diner, as I'm sure you could tell. Stella, I don't need the pay, that's not the issue, but I'm losing my damn mind. Let me fill in for Jackson, just until he's back on his feet. It would give me a reason to get out of bed. I promise, I'll stay out of your way."

He had no intention of doing that, but she didn't need to know all his secrets.

"Liam, I—"

"Before you say no, think about it. You can pay Jackson for the hours I work. I'm sure it would help with the ER bill. I need something to do with my time, and this happens to be my area of expertise. It's a win-win for everyone." It was perilous pointing out the simple fact he would be helping her out of a bind too, but a risk he had to take.

She was quiet for so long he was afraid his plan wasn't going to work. "I can't let you work and not pay you something."

"Think of it like an internship, except you're getting a more experienced intern than some high school kid."

Stella stood from her chair, and Liam followed suit, certain she was about to show him the door.

"You'll report to Whitney. She'll give you all the information you need based on the excursion. Any questions you have will go to her. That's how things work with Jackson, and that's how they'll stay."

"You have no idea how much I appreciate this, Stel."

The thought resonated in his soul. No matter the reason he'd come here, the truth was, he was suddenly more excited about the opportunity to do what he loved than he thought he would be. It had been months since he'd led a team on any kind of adventure.

When he'd agreed to stay on until the sale of his company was final, Liam had assumed he would continue running trips as usual, but that hadn't been the case. Instead, the final two months had been spent with the new CEO going over all the ins and outs of the business.

Until then, Liam hadn't realized the extent of the mess his ex-partner had made. He'd known the financials were a mess, but it went well beyond that. He might miss the adventure, but he would never miss the business end of owning a company.

He didn't have a clue where his life was headed but the idea of working, and helping Stella out at the same time, felt promising.

"Liam."

He locked eyes with Stella's soft green gaze. "Yeah?"

"Don't make me regret this." And with that, she turned and walked out of the conference room.

Liam's lips turned up into a smile. If he had any say over it, she wouldn't regret a single moment they spent together.

Chapter Seven

Liam woke Saturday morning feeling like a new man. The sun was shining, the high was supposed to hit eighty, and he had a job to do.

To the average thirty-five-year-old man, spending a Friday night going through boxes to find gear would have been the lamest of the lame, but for Liam it had been the most exciting thing he'd done since he returned.

Well, maybe not the *most* exciting.

Sleeping with Stella undeniably took first place, but prepping for a guide definitely took second place. It wasn't exactly a testament to an exciting life, but with a little luck, his social calendar was about to change.

Rolling out of bed, Liam walked to the kitchen, and popped a K-cup in the Keurig. His tiny apartment was still cluttered with boxes and looked like an episode of Hoarders, but until he figured out a more permanent solution for housing, unpacking was not on the priority list. What was the use in dragging everything out just to box it up again?

He had his clothes and coffee maker, what more did a man need?

With his cup full, Liam poured in two creamers and headed back toward the bathroom for a quick shower. The last thing he wanted was to be late for his first gig. He knew he was on thin ice with Stella, and pissing off his new boss would not bode well.

Boss. He let the word roll around on his tongue.

Stella James was—for all intents and purposes—his boss. Why in the hell did the thought of her bossing him around turn him on so damn much?

Tucking that thought away for later examination, Liam showered quickly, and then threw on a pair of board shorts and a t-shirt with a sweatshirt over top. He had no intention of getting in the water this early in the season, but he needed to be prepared in case someone else went in. They wouldn't be happy once they felt the cold temps of the water, but it was always a possibility with inexperienced kayakers.

From what Whitney had told him yesterday, the nine guests he was taking out today were all high-level employees from a tech company out of Atlanta, here on an executive retreat. His job was to lead them through the marsh area known as Battery Creek, and make sure they all returned safe and happy.

Easy enough.

Liam arrived at Pebble Creek Plantation ten minutes ahead of schedule thanks to the non-existent traffic in Beaufort County. Pulling into the drive, he parked his truck and headed in through the front door. The sound of laughter and easy conversation drifted from the kitchen where he assumed his group for the day was finishing up their breakfast.

"Good, you're early." Whitney greeted him as he entered the conference room.

To his dismay, Stella was nowhere in sight. "Good morning to you, too."

"Sorry, mornings aren't my strong suit." Whitney smiled. "Follow me, we'll go load up. I just need to grab one thing from Stella's office first."

Liam followed Whitney as she headed down the hallway toward the office.

"Hey, Liam from Colorado." Willa popped up from her seat on the couch. "Aunt Whit said you were helping out."

Aunt Whit? Stella was an only child. Did that mean Whitney was the sister of Willa's dad? Was Stella in business with her, well, not quite in-laws?

Whitney's voice interrupted his musing. "Crap, I swear I would lose my head if it weren't attached some days. Hangout here one sec, I'll be right back."

"Mornings aren't your strong suit, got it." Liam smiled.

"You're witty. I like you a little more already." Whitney smiled before heading back out through the office door.

"She's not my real aunt, if that's what you were wondering."

Damn, maybe the kid was psychic, not smart. "Oh. Is your mom here?"

"You ask a lot of questions about my mom, old friend Liam." Willa cocked her head at him.

"Do you always call people by their name and how you know them?" Liam returned a cocked brow at her.

"I like to give people nicknames, but I don't know you well enough to pick one for you yet." Willa shrugged. "My mom is at home setting up for the party. You should come. All the employees will be there."

"What kind of party?" Liam asked, his curiosity getting the best of him.

"The kind where you grill hamburgers and hotdogs, and everyone that works for my mom will be there."

"That's nice of you to offer, but I'm only helping out temporarily. I don't think I count as a real employee." Except, if it meant going to a cookout where Stella would be, he wanted to count. His plan was shit if he couldn't spend time with Stella.

"It's at our house. Seventeen twenty-three Stonewall, if you change your mind." Willa spoke the address quickly.

Liam could sense the urgency in her words as Whitney's footsteps echoed down the hall. He had a feeling he wasn't invited on purpose, and not just because he was the temporary help filling in, but the idea of seeing where Stella lived was suddenly tempting.

He'd wondered a lot about her life over the years. Where she was living? What she was up to? Was she happy? There were still so many unanswered questions, and Willa had given him an in.

There was a good chance Stella would be pissed if he showed up, but it was a cookout for her employees, and she was the one who insisted on paying him. How mad could she be?

*****

Stella stared out over her backyard with a nagging feeling something was off. The bounce house was set up and ready to go, check. The decorations were hung, check. The food was prepped and ready to go on the grill, check. Hopefully, whatever it was, would come to her before the guests started arriving.

Stella turned and faced her best friend who was currently lounging in one of the patio chairs. "Why is it that I can plan parties that cost tens of thousands of dollars in my sleep, but a nine-year-old's birthday party feels like it's going to be the death of me?"

"Because you stress too much about Willa's happiness. She's good, James. She's the happiest kid I know." Whitney flashed her a genuine smile.

"It's just...I don't want her to always be the *different* kid."

"Stella, I get that you worry about her, but she's good. She's happy. She has friends. So what if she's the smart one? When she gets to high school, she can start a tutoring service."

"You're always my eternal optimist." Stella laughed. "Speaking of your optimism, how did it go this morning?"

"Honestly, he's a natural with people. He was charming the CEO before they got in the van to head out. I have no doubt it will be a successful excursion."

A swirl of emotion churned in her chest. This account was important to her, and trusting Liam with her business was not easy. "Good. That's good."

"You know, having someone of Liam's caliber could be a real asset to our operation." Whitney stood from her seat. "We could expand things. Offer more packages. Jackson's great, don't get me wrong, but he's a twenty-two-year-old kid who's living his best life. He's not a businessman."

If it were anyone other than her ex she would agree whole-heartedly, but having Liam around was a detriment to her health. "There's too much water under that bridge."

"There's never too much water. Just build a bigger bridge. I know you guys had a thing way back when, but this is business. You're always putting the business first, why not now?"

This was not the time or place for this conversation. "Let it go, Whit."

"Am I interrupting?"

Both women turned to see Rick stepping out onto the back porch.

"No." Stella leaned in and hugged him. "Just some work talk, but it's time for the party and that can wait."

"Good to see you, Rick." Whitney gave him a quick wave.

"There was another car pulling up when I came in." Rick threw his thumb back toward the house. "Should I get the birthday girl?"

Stella returned his smile though it was forced. "That would be great. She's in her room. When you get back, would you mind helping me with the grill?"

"Of course." Rick pressed a soft kiss to her forehead and headed back into the house.

From over her shoulder, Stella heard the soft snort coming from Whitney. "What?"

"You've got to stop stringing that poor man along."

"I'm not stringing him anywhere. He's Willa's dad, what am I supposed to do?"

"For starters, stop using him as a shield for every other man out there. You're young and beautiful. It's time to get back on the horse."

"I'm not using him as a shield." Except that's exactly what she was doing. Rick was her safe zone. "And I don't have time to go on horrendous first dates. I have a business to run."

"They're not all horrendous." Whitney shook her head. "You're just scared you might find someone decent."

"What is this, pick on Stella day? You do remember I'm the one you come complaining to every time you go out with one of your online dates and it ends terribly. What about the fast-food guy who wanted to share a drink so he didn't have to buy a second one?"

"Hey!" Whitney laughed. "He had a valid point. Drinks are overpriced."

"Whit, he took you to a fast-food joint. He couldn't spring for his own drink?"

"The point is, they're not all bad." Whitney stood and wrapped her arm around Stella's shoulders. "It's time to open up Stellaland to the public."

"Oh my God, stop. I have a party to host, and we are not comparing my body to a theme park." Stella slipped from her best friend's hold and headed toward the guests coming through the side gate.

"It's time for a grand opening," Whitney called across the yard.

By one o'clock, the party was in full swing. Shrills and giggles billowed out of the bounce house as the smell of burgers filled the air. Stella couldn't have asked for a better day if she'd tried. The sun was shining bright, as a light breeze blew through the yard. It was perfect.

Everything was perfect.

"Pardon me ladies, I need to go check on lunch." Stella excused herself from the group of moms she'd been chatting with, and headed across the yard toward the deck where Rick was manning the grill.

Just as she stepped into the shade of the old oak tree, the side gate opened, and her heart dropped. Standing in the opening, Liam twisted his face into a look of confusion. Stella's eyes darted to Whitney who was oblivious to what was happening.

Walking over to her quickly, Stella gently wrapped her hand around Whitney's arm. "Can I borrow you for a second?"

"Yeah, sure." As they stepped away from the other Pebble Creek employees, Whitney spoke under her breath. "Okay, what's the crisis?"

Stella stopped in her tracks. "What's he doing here, Whit?"

"Who?" Whitney spun and Stella knew the moment her eyes locked on Liam. "Oh!"

"This isn't a game, Whitney. What? You thought if you invited him to Willa's party, I would see how charming he was, and hire him on full time?"

Whitney's eyes grew wide. "Wait, you think I invited him?"

"Well, if you didn't invite him then who did?"

Before Whitney could answer, Stella heard Willa's voice call across the backyard. "Liam, you came!"

"Well." Whitney snickered. "Guess that answers that question."

"This is not funny. How did this happen?"

"I don't know. I just…"

"What? You what?" Stella asked in a rush.

"I left them alone for two minutes. I forgot the van keys in the kitchen and went to grab them. Willa must have asked him to come."

Stella's blood pressure hit the roof. What had gotten into her daughter? This wasn't like Willa to invite someone without asking.

"Do you want me to handle it?" Whitney asked.

80

"No." It wasn't exactly the truth. Stella would much rather have Whitney send him on his way than have to deal with the situation. Having Liam here at her house made her nervous for reasons she didn't want to examine, but she couldn't pawn her problems off on Whitney. "I'll talk to him."

Mustering the small shred of courage she could gather, Stella crossed the yard to face the past that was hell-bent on being in the present.

Chapter Eight

Liam had hustled a fair amount of people to get ahead, but he may have met his match when it came to Willa James.

Standing in the open gate, he took in the sight before him. His ego and desire had led him straight into the depths of a kid's birthday party. He'd been so focused on trying to spend time with Stella that he had ignored the red flags. Willa waiting until they were alone to mention the party. Her hurried speech when she'd heard Whitney returning.

Based on the inflated balloon in the shape of a nine, he'd been manipulated by a girl still in the single digits.

He should leave. Turn around and pretend this never happened.

"Liam, you came!"

Shit. He'd hesitated too long, and now he'd been spotted.

"Hey there, Birthday Girl." Liam smiled down as Willa approached. "You forgot to mention the part about this being your birthday party."

"Did I?" Willa shrugged.

So, she knew what she was doing. Duly noted. He was going to have to be more careful with this kid, before she landed him on the wrong side of Stella.

"I'm on to you." Liam scrubbed a hand across her staticky hair. "Listen, I appreciate the invite but I'm not sure your mom would want me at your party. Go have fun with your friends and have a good birthday."

"No, you don't have to go. Look, all the other staff is here." Liam looked up to follow her line of sight, but his eyes locked on Stella. She was headed right for them. "Mom, tell Liam he doesn't have to go."

Stella stopped next to her daughter. "Willa, go back to your friends while I talk to Liam."

The young girl crossed her arms over her chest. "You're going to make him leave, aren't you?"

"Willa James." Stella's voice was firm, but somehow still warm.

Liam leaned down, getting on eye level with Willa. "It's no fun if you get in trouble at your birthday party. Listen to your mom and go play."

"Fine." Willa huffed, but she turned and trotted off to the bounce house.

"I don't need your help parenting." It was Stella's turn to cross her arms and huff.

"Stel, I'm not trying...I didn't know it was her birthday party. I never would have come."

Liam had never felt more like an ass in his life. First, he crashed a party he wasn't invited to, and now she thought he was trying to parent her kid. His perfect day had taken a hard right turn, right off the edge of a cliff.

The paddle down Battery Creek had been the most fun he'd had working in months. Being out on the water, laughing with a group of perfect strangers, had lifted a weight off his shoulders. It wasn't a permanent gig, he knew that, but it reminded him why he'd started his company in the first place. He loved meeting people from all walks of life, and sharing adventures with them.

Now, he just felt like he was up Shit Creek without a paddle.

"Anyway, you have a party to get back to. I'm sorry I interrupted." Liam turned to go, not bothering to say goodbye.

"Wait." Stella's soft voice stopped him in his tracks. "What exactly did she tell you?"

Liam rubbed a hand across the back of his neck. The last thing he wanted was to cause problems between Stella and her daughter, or get the kid in trouble. "It doesn't matter. If you need me to cover any other trips, just have Whitney call me."

"Liam…"

There was a vulnerability in her voice that pulled at his heart. "It's okay, Stella."

"No, it's not." She let out a heavy sigh. "You can't leave."

Stella didn't want him there, that much was clear, and yet she was asking him to stay. Why? "I don't understand."

"She invited you, and you're here now. If I kick you out that makes me the bad guy, and I can't be the bad guy today. I don't expect you to understand. You asked me to do you a favor and let you take on Jackson's job while he recovers. Now, I need a favor from you."

"Okay. Anything." Liam took a step closer. It was reckless and dumb, but God he'd do anything to get in Stella's good graces.

"For reasons I may never understand, Willa has taken to you. I need you to keep your distance. She may be a genius when it comes to some things, but emotionally, she's still a nine-year-old. And I'm not about to drag her into our complicated past."

"Stella…I can't change the past, but our future doesn't have to be complicated."

Stella's arms slipped free from across her chest, as a curt laugh crossed her lips. "We don't have a future, Liam."

"That's not what I meant." Lies, it was exactly what he meant. He wasn't trying to walk her down the aisle, but he would definitely be on board with another midnight adventure. "I meant we can be friends again."

Liam glanced over Stella's shoulder as a man he'd never seen approached.

"Everything good here?" The man let his hands rest on Stella's shoulders. They were comfortable with each other, that much was evident.

"Of course." Stella's face morphed back into that perfectly crafted smile he'd seen at the wedding. It wasn't her real smile, but rather the one she used to convince the world she had her life together. "Rick, this is Liam. He's helping fill in while Jackson recovers. Liam, this is Rick. Willa's father."

Liam had never considered himself a jealous man, but at that moment, the unwanted emotion swirled with disappointment in his gut.

"Nice to meet you, Liam." Rick extended his hand out for a quick shake before turning back to Stella. "The food is ready if you want to call everyone up. I'll go get our birthday girl."

Our. The word reverberated in Liam's tight chest.

So, Stella was involved with someone. It shouldn't have come as a surprise the girl he'd fallen in love with years ago had moved on, and yet, he felt like he'd been kneed in the stomach.

"You should probably get back to your…" He couldn't bring himself to say the word lingering on his tongue. "To Rick, I mean."

As unhealthy as it was, he couldn't help but wonder what kind of relationship Stella had with the man. She hadn't introduced him as her boyfriend, husband, hell, not even her ex. Only as Willa's father.

A burning curiosity needed to know exactly what kind of relationship they had. They'd obviously been together at some point. Were they divorced? He'd never seen Stella wear a ring, so he was pretty confident they weren't currently married. Then again, for all he knew they could still be legally married, and trying to work things out. Maybe they were in the midst of being separated and that's why she didn't have a thin piece of metal wrapped around her ring finger.

It's none of your concern.

A tiny voice of reason tried to work its way through the maddening thoughts, but it was too late. Liam needed to know what the story was between Stella and this man.

"Liam, I..." Stella glanced over her shoulder and then back to him.

Liam sensed her hesitation, which only added to the rampant thoughts flowing through his mind. There were so many things he wanted to know, but this wasn't the time or place. "It's okay. I get it."

Honestly, he didn't get a damn thing that was happening in that moment, but the words seemed to satisfy whatever thought was on her mind. As she walked away, he couldn't help but feel a sense of déjà vu. Maybe this was all they were ever meant to be. Two people who were terrible at communicating, but stellar at walking away from each other.

There is no future for us. Stella's words echoed in his mind.

He'd been a fool to think he could show up at some party and sweep her off her feet. Stella had moved on. She'd built a life for herself while he'd been out sowing his wild oats. Whatever he thought he was after, he was too late.

Too late and stuck at a little girl's birthday party.

If he left now, Willa would think her mom made him go. And the last thing he wanted was to cause any more trouble. Stella was wrong about one thing, he completely understood not wanting to be the bad guy. He didn't want to disappoint Willa on her birthday any more than her mom did. He would just have to bide a little time until he could slip out without anyone noticing.

For thirty minutes, Liam sat in the shade of the oak tree and tried his damnedest to ignore Stella's laugh every time Slick Rick spoke. The Stella he remembered had stood on her own two feet and hadn't needed the attention or approval of any man. The Stella up on the porch, however, seemed to cling to every word her boyfriend had to say.

Liam pulled his attention away from the porch as Whitney took a seat next to him.

"You should get something to eat. There's plenty up there." Whitney sat her plate on her lap and lowered her cup to the ground.

"I'm fine, thanks." There was no way in hell he was going up on that porch. The Stella and Rick show was bad enough from the lawn, he didn't need a front-row seat. Liam shifted in his seat to face Whitney. "Can I ask you something?"

"Sure." Whitney flashed him a smile. "As long as I can answer between bites. I'm starving."

Liam held up his hands in a sign of surrender. "I would never get between a hungry woman and her food."

Whitney's smile grew wider. "You're a smart man."

"Well, I don't know about that, I did get conned into a little girl's birthday party. Speaking of which, what's the acceptable amount of time one has to stay at a party before slipping quietly out the back?"

Whitney finished chewing. "That bad, huh?"

"I'm not sure awkward covers how uncomfortable this is. Don't get me wrong, it's a very nice party, but the invitation didn't exactly specify it was for a nine-year-old."

"I get it." Whitney laughed. "I've been bamboozled a time or two by that nine-year-old. You learn to ask the right questions."

"Apparently not my strong suit." Liam shook his head.

"If it's any consolation, you only look mildly in pain."

It was Liam's turn to laugh. "Thanks…I think."

"You're probably safe to sneak out at any point, but I would recommend waiting for cake time. Everyone will be distracted, and no one will notice you making a run for it."

"Look who's the smart one now. Wanna make a break for it with me? I would say you could bring the rest of the staff, but people will notice a mass exodus."

"As the godmother, I'm obligated to see it through to the end, but I like your solidarity."

"Tough gig." Liam shrugged and flashed her a playful smile.

"Nah, it's not so bad. She's a good kid. So, my turn to ask you a question."

Liam hesitated, feigning a look of concern. "I'm not sure I can handle questions from the fairy godmother."

"Don't worry, I left my wand at home." Whitney winked. "How do you feel about deep-sea fishing?"

"Are you asking me on a date? Because I have to say, I'm a little suspicious of women who want to take me out in the middle of the ocean on a first date."

"Smart, cute, and funny. Aren't you just the holy trinity?"

"So, you're not asking me on a date to the middle of the Atlantic?"

"The Stanley Group is going deep-sea fishing on Monday. Technically, the company we chartered with will handle the trip, but we usually send Jackson to keep up our professional relationship with the clients. They seemed to take to you this morning. You're good with people. Dare I say, charismatic."

"You think I'm smart, cute, funny, and smooth. You might be my soulmate. Any chance you want to grab a beer after this and discuss our future?" Liam arched a brow.

Whitney covered her mouth to hide her laughter. "Does that line work for you?"

Liam held a hand to his chest. "Now you're just bruising my ego."

"Something tells me you're not that wounded. After all, we both know I'm not the woman you were hoping to score a date with." Whitney tilted her head, daring him to disagree.

—

90

"Maybe not, but I see the other ship has sailed, so you can't blame a guy for asking a beautiful woman to have a beer with him."

Whitney wasn't wrong. Stella was the only reason he'd shown up in the first place, but he wasn't wrong either. Stella had no interest in taking a stroll down Nostalgia Lane with him.

"In a different world, I think you and I could have some real fun, but I draw the line at fraternizing with my best friend's whatever…" Whitney let her words drift as she waved a hand in his direction.

Liam studied her for a moment before responding. "You're fishing. She never told you about us."

"Not exactly, but what I do know is that I've never seen that woman so unraveled in all the years I've known her. You make her nervous, which says a lot."

"Maybe all my charisma is just overwhelming." He doubted it was nerves Whitney was sensing, and more like annoyance.

"Look, whatever happened between you two was obviously a long time ago, so let me offer you some current advice. Stella doesn't do spontaneity or whims, despite what may have happened at your brother's wedding. Which is shocking by the way and probably deserves better examination, but for the record, she thought you were leaving. If you want a shot with her, and I think you should, you have to be patient."

It was apparent Whitney was a glass half full kind of girl, but a little positive thinking wasn't going to change Stella's mind. That bridge had been burned from both ends and they were standing on opposite banks. "I appreciate the advice, but I think we're a little past patience and positivity. Besides, she seems a little preoccupied."

Before Whitney could utter a response, a chorus of young voices filled the air as the kids gathered around the cake.

"Well, I guess that's your cue." Whitney winked and stood from her chair. "I'll go distract the masses with cake while you make a run for it."

It was his cue indeed.

Liam watched as Stella and Rick stood behind their daughter. He wasn't sure what the deal was between them, but they were a family unit. Coming here had been a mistake.

Hell, thinking he could walk back into Stella's life was a mistake.

What had happened between them a week ago had meant nothing to her. She'd only slept with him because she'd thought he would be gone. She had Willa and Rick. She had her business. Beyond filling in for Jackson, she didn't need him.

He'd convinced Stella to give him the gig, and he would see it through. If she'd had any other option, she wouldn't have given him the job which meant he wouldn't leave her in the lurch. But more importantly, it was the closest thing to his old life he'd done in months. The trip out this morning had felt amazing, and he wasn't ready to give it up. He would show up when Whitney called and nothing more.

Liam followed Whitney across the lawn toward the gate he'd entered an hour earlier with his head hung low. For the day to have started out so well, this wasn't how he'd hoped it would end. Lost in thought, he nearly plowed into Whitney when she stopped short and turned to face him.

Before he could utter an apology for nearly trampling her, Whitney lifted up on her tiptoes and planted a kiss on his cheek.

"You can't always believe what you see." Whitney winked and patted him on the chest. "See you Monday, Scott. Seven a.m."

What the hell just happened?

Chapter Nine

Stella was going to need a nap by the time the party ended. As if hosting a gaggle of eight and nine-year-olds wasn't exhausting enough, having to mentally block out thoughts of Liam in her personal space was downright draining.

Secretly, there was a part of her that wanted to know what he thought about her home and the life she'd built, but going down that road would never end well.

"You can give up the Rick ruse now."

Stella turned to find her best friend standing in the doorway of her kitchen. "I don't know what you're talking about."

Ignoring Whitney's grin, Stella continued loading the dishwasher with serving utensils and platters. A smarter mom would have used disposable products for the food display, but the event host in her couldn't do it. At least she'd used plastic for the plates and cups.

Lunch had been served, and the cake had been cut. All she had to do was get through presents, and she would be in the clear.

"Right, because you always cling to Ranger Rick like white on rice." Whitney stepped in and closed the sliding glass door behind her.

"Shhh, he's right outside on the porch." Stella glanced out to make sure Rick hadn't heard Whitney. "And I am not clinging to him."

"I haven't seen you this flirtatious in...ever. Anyway, I thought I would let you know Liam left."

Stella expected to feel a sense of relief at the news, but a different wave of emotion washed over her entirely. From the moment Liam Scott had walked back into her life, she'd felt anything but relief. She'd never been so unsure and unsteady in her life, and it was all because of the sex.

The terrifically, amazing, aerobic sex.

It was messing with her head. How the hell was she supposed to be steady and strong when the man kept giving her the *I've seen you naked* look?

"I never should've slept with him." Stella blurted the words without thinking.

"I'm going to need you to be a little more specific about which *him*." Whitney's lips turned up into a smirk. "The one you said you didn't sleep with or the one you've been pretending to be madly in love with for the past hour?"

Stella cut her eyes at her best friend. Whitney wasn't dumb. She knew exactly who *he* was, she just wanted to hear Stella say it out loud. "I'm not dignifying that question with an answer."

"I hate to break it to you, but I think your dignity checked out roughly fifty-three minutes ago, give or take."

"Can you add *find a new best friend and assistant* to my calendar for Monday?" Stella rolled her eyes like a sixteen-year-old.

Of course, the eye rolling was par for the course considering she'd been acting like a teenager from the moment Liam stepped into her backyard.

"I would, but you're going to be hard pressed to find someone who can fill these size eights." Whitney moved across the kitchen and leaned against the counter next to Stella. "Look, you had some amazing sex with a guy you used to know. It's not a big deal. A lot of women like to *reminisce* with an old partner, but it doesn't have to mean anything. It's only as awkward as you make it."

"I never said it was amazing." Stella huffed.

"Oh, your actions are screaming amazing sex loud and clear. No one acts like a fool over bad sex. I mean, honestly, if it was that good, I'm not sure why you don't reminisce a little more." Whitney bumped her shoulder against Stella's.

"Liam's more than just some guy I used to date." Stella hesitated, afraid to say the words out loud in her own home. "He was the love of my life and then…he left. He quit loving me back."

"I hate to break it to you, James, but that man has not stopped loving you."

"You don't know what you're talking about." This was not the conversation she wanted to be having with Whitney. Not now, not ever. Liam was her past, not her future. That bridge had gone up in flames.

"He sat through a little girl's birthday party, watching the one person he came to see flirting with another man, just so Willa wouldn't think you were the bad guy. And despite the fact he thinks this ship has sailed, he's going to keep showing up to work because he doesn't want to disappoint you. He's pulling his hat out of the ring and ignoring his own feelings because he thinks it's what's best for you. Tell me that isn't a man with a bulldozer full of feelings?"

"Leave it alone, Whit."

"All I'm saying—"

"Stop." Stella cut her off before she could say anything else. "I don't know why Liam showed up here today or what he's up to, but he's right about one thing, this ship sailed a long time ago. The moment he walked out on our engagement."

"You two were engaged?" Whitney's voice was colored with shock. "Why didn't you tell me?"

"Like I said, it was a long time ago." Stella closed her eyes and drew in a deep breath.

Leave it in the past. She repeated the mantra that had been stuck in her head like a broken record for the past week.

Whitney was wrong. There was no way Liam was still in love with her.

But what if he was?

No, it wasn't possible. He may be in lust, but he wasn't in love. It had been twelve years. No one hung on that long.

And even if he thought he loved her, she didn't care. She had moved on. She had Willa. She had Whitney and her business. She had everything she needed.

Liam had a chance, but he hadn't wanted it. He'd thrown it away. Just like her father, Liam had walked out on his promises. It's what the men in her life did. Promise the world, and then rip it all away.

Whatever game Liam Scott was playing, she wasn't rolling the dice…but damn if she didn't want to.

*****

"How's my perfect little niece?" Liam spoke softly as he walked into his sister's living room, and sat next to Kat on the couch.

"She's completely rotten and opposed to the idea of sleeping without being held, but otherwise she's absolutely perfect."

"Looks like her dad doesn't have a problem sleeping." Liam glanced over to Brooks asleep in the recliner with their daughter snuggled against his chest.

Brooks cracked one eye open and whispered. "I can hear you. I was just trying to trick her into a nap by pretending I was asleep, too."

"How's that going?" Liam chuckled softly.

"Like a charm, but I think I fell asleep first."

"She sleeps well to the sound of his snoring," Kat ribbed her husband.

"Whatever works, I'll take it. I've never been so tired in my life."

"Why don't you let me take her next door for a few hours and you two can sleep?" The words were out of Liam's mouth before he thought about what he was saying. He didn't know the first thing about babies, but it couldn't be that hard.

"It's Saturday night." Kat gave him a quizzical look. "I'm sure you have something better to do than babysit so we can take a nap."

The sad truth was he didn't have a damn thing to do.

After slipping out of Willa's party, he'd stopped for lunch at the diner, and then headed home to shower. He'd wasted a few hours between Netflix and his phone before deciding to call his younger brother, Drew. Only, his little brother had a hot date.

Next up, he'd called Carter, but the baby of their family was on the way to the airport in Charleston. Miles and Julia were due back from their honeymoon around eight. Had Liam known earlier, he would have offered to ride with Carter, but his brother was already in route.

With all his brothers occupied, Liam was left between spending the evening with his parents or Kat and her newborn, and he wasn't ready to admit his best option was hanging out with his parents on a Saturday night.

He needed some damn friends, stat.

With only one real option, Liam had headed down his steps and across the yard to Kat's, but now that he was here, his sister and brother-in-law looked like walking zombies that could keel over any minute.

"I'm serious," Liam continued. "I can take Penelope over to my place and you two can get a couple hours of uninterrupted sleep. I'll be right next door if I need anything, but I'm sure we'll be fine. How hard can it be?"

Kat's laughter filled the room causing her daughter to stir. "Okay, now I wanna say yes just to see how long it takes you to tap out."

"I say let him." Brooks joined in on Kat's laughter. "I give him forty-five minutes at best. It's almost the witching hour."

"Wait, what's the witching hour?" Liam felt his gut tighten.

"Nothing you can't handle." Kat patted him on the arm. "It's almost time for me to nurse her anyway, then she shouldn't need to eat for a few hours."

"So that's a yes?"

"Maybe it's the exhaustion talking, but sure, why not." Kat stood from the couch. "Let me get some stuff together and then I'll feed her."

What the hell had Liam gotten himself into? At the rate he was going, he was going to wear a hole in his carpet from the pacing, or need a total knee replacement from all the bouncing. It was really a tossup at the moment.

Witching hour, his ass, it should be called the Devil's hour.

"Honestly, how can so much noise come from one tiny human?" Liam looked down at his niece who had obviously been possessed by a demon for the last ten minutes. "All right, we can do this. We are not calling your mom. She thinks Uncle Liam can't do this and we're going to prove her wrong. Okay?"

As though she refused his plan, Penelope let out a loud cry.

"That doesn't really sound like you're on board." Liam bounced and moved around the room. "We've got this, I promise. You're dry. Your mom fed you, which is great because I can't help you out there, Kid. Now, I just need you to stop crying or wear yourself out…whichever feels right for you."

The answering scream grated across his nerve endings.

"Fine, new plan. Mommy and Daddy are taking a little nap, and we can't call grandma because she'll tell mommy I suck at this, so who else can we call?"

Pulling out his phone, Liam opened up his recent contacts and spotted Whitney's number. She didn't have kids of her own that he knew of, but she was a woman and Willa's godmother, so she had to have some motherly instincts, right?

Tapping her name, Liam lifted the phone to his ear.

"Liam, hey…is that a baby crying?"

"Whitney, hi. Umm, I was wondering if you maybe knew how to exorcise a demon from a newborn?"

Laughter swirled in his ear. "What? Why do you have a baby?"

"She's my niece, and apparently it's the witching hour or whatever, but I think it might be more like demons rather than witches. I've tried all the things my sister said, but nothing is working. Maybe you could come wave your fairy godmother wand and make it stop."

"You know, I'm not actually a fairy godmother. There is no magic wand."

"Right, no magic wand." Liam let out a heavy sigh. "You wouldn't happen to be a baby whisperer, would you?"

Whitney's answering laugh filled his ear again. "Not exactly, but hang on, I have something better than my proverbial wand."

Like he had any other options than to hang on. If Whitney had some magic trick up her sleeve, he would take it. Hell, he'd take an asteroid to the ear at the moment.

"Hello."

Liam froze mid pace at the voice coming through the phone. "Stella?"

Muffled voices filtered through the phone before Stella came back on the line. "Tell me what you've tried?"

"Everything. I've bounced, I've sung, shamelessly begged. Nothing has worked. Please tell me you have some secret mom code to turn it off?"

A soft chuckle flowed through the phone. "There is no secret mom code. Have you called Kat?"

"No and that's not an option. She already thinks I can't handle this."

"There's no shame in throwing in the towel."

Liam could feel his frustration taking over. His nerves were shot from the non-stop cry fest, and he didn't need another woman telling him he couldn't handle this. "Kat's exhausted and I'm trying to let her get some sleep. If you're not going to help, I'm hanging up. We'll figure this out."

The silence through the phone would have been deafening if not for the screaming nine pounds in his arms. Pulling the phone away from his ear, Liam looked to see if the call was still connected.

"Text me your address."

"What?" Liam couldn't believe the words he was hearing.

"Text me the address before I change my mind."

"What about Willa?"

"She's having a sleepover with Whitney. Just text me the address."

Liam listened as the three little beeps signaled the end of the call. As much as he needed the help, he needed to keep his distance. Stella had been clear there was no place for him in her world. No future to be had.

Looking down at his unhappy niece, uncertainty rolled through him. He needed help even if it came in all the wrong packaging. Texting the address to Whitney's phone, Liam slipped his phone back in his pocket.

"Listen Pen, help is on the way, but you have to promise to be a good buffer. You have to promise to not let Uncle Liam screw this up more."

Chapter Ten

There were bad ideas and then there were absurdly insane ideas. Going to Liam's apartment alone on a Saturday night was definitely verging on complete insanity.

In the dim glow of her interior lights, Stella checked her reflection in the rearview mirror and sighed. It didn't matter what she looked like. She wasn't here for a date. She was here to offer a hand to a friend. That was it.

Friend. The label rolled through her mind like a freight train.

Could she be friends with Liam? She'd been very clear that there was no future for the two of them, but she wasn't sure how she felt about being friends with her ex. Liam had been nothing but kind to her since his return, offering to help out at Pebble Creek in Jackson's absence, and staying at Willa's party for her benefit even after she'd been a complete bitch to him.

But friends?

It felt like a slippery slope. She could blame the wine all she wanted for their night in the boat house, but the truth was she'd been aware of the choice she was making—even if she'd thought he'd be a million miles away from here by now. And worse than the fact that she'd slept with him, she'd enjoyed it.

Really enjoyed it.

Like riding a bike, she'd hopped right back on and taken him for a spin as though no time had passed. Now, all she could think about was taking another damn ride. Seven days later and every time she closed her eyes, she could still feel his fingers grazing across her skin.

It was the sole reason she'd clung to Rick during the party. Trusting herself to behave in Liam's presence was not something she was confident she could do. And yet here she was, outside his house.

If she were a stronger woman maybe friends with benefits could be an option, but that was more complicated than her heart could handle. Which was really too bad, because if there was anything Liam was gifted at, it was sex.

"This is a terrible idea." Stella's words drifted through the empty car.

Whether she was referring to helping Liam or being his friend, she wasn't sure. Maybe it was to both.

As she wrestled with her indecision, the sound of an incoming text startled her. Grabbing her phone from the seat next to her, Stella immediately regretted checking the message.

Don't be a chickenshit.

Tapping the screen, she typed out a quick response to Whitney.

You have such a way with words.

Before her best friend could respond with more eloquent words of wisdom, Stella placed her phone on silent. She didn't need comments from the peanut gallery. If she listened to Whitney's dating advice, Stella would have a harem of men at her disposal every day of the week. Not something she was interested in.

Pulling herself together, Stella stepped out of the car, and made her way up the driveway toward the set of stairs on the outside of the garage. As she reached the top landing, the sight of Liam swaying in the middle of the small apartment took her breath away. From the looks of it, he'd won the battle, but the war had been hell.

Never in her life had she seen him so disheveled. His standard composure lost to the messy hair, wide eyes, and sweat stains under his arms. He looked like he'd gone to battle and barely survived.

But for all his dishevelment, there was also something quite beautiful about him. The tender way he held his niece. The adoration and protection scrunched in his brow. That little girl was going to be loved with the force of a thousand storms.

Moisture puddled in the corner of her eyes. She should leave now. She could text him from the car that something came up and she wouldn't be able to make it. It wasn't like he needed her any longer.

Except, now that she was here, watching him in this vulnerable moment, she didn't want to leave. She couldn't quite put her finger on it, but something was different about the man standing twenty feet from her.

Friends? She let the idea swirl around her mind again.

Maybe it wasn't a complete impossibility. There would definitely be no benefits, but friends didn't feel completely off the table.

Not wanting to wake the sleeping beauty, Stella opened the door slowly and let herself in. Two bright green eyes flashed up at her, but she held a finger to her lips and pulled out her phone. Opening an app, she pulled up the video that had saved her life when Willa was a baby. Eight hours of continuous vacuum noise. It sounded crazy, but it had worked like a charm every time.

Motioning for Liam to follow her, she walked over to the only visible door in the apartment. As suspected, his bedroom lay beyond the opening. Stella crossed the room and switched on the small bedside lamp.

"Lay her on her back gently in the middle," she whispered softly as she laid her phone on the bed.

"What if she rolls off?" Liam's eyes grew wide with panic.

Stella smiled and rested a hand on his bicep before speaking quietly. "She's a week old. She's not rolling anywhere."

She watched in awe as Liam leaned over and gingerly placed his niece on top of the navy comforter. It took all her strength not to react when the tiny girl let out a grunt and he nearly abandoned the plan. Holding in her laughter, Stella patted the baby's hip gently as the infant settled in the queen-sized bed.

When she seemed to be fast asleep, Stella took a small step back from the bed. "We should let her sleep." Her voice was barely a whisper over the soft noise coming from her phone.

"I can't leave her. Kat would kill me." Liam's eyes were full of worry.

Smiling, Stella pointed toward the open wall across the small room. "Come on, let's sit down. You look like you might pass out at any moment."

"I look that bad, huh?" Liam followed her across the room.

"Just a little worse for the wear." Stella took a seat on the soft carpet and leaned against the wall.

Liam followed suit and sat next to her, keeping his voice low. "Good to see honesty is still one of your core values."

"It's endearing."

Liam cocked a brow at her. "Your honesty or me looking like a disaster?"

Stella couldn't stop the smile from spreading across her face if she wanted to. "You taking care of your niece so your sister can get some rest. It's sweet."

"Yeah, well, you can't tell anyone. I don't want anyone thinking I've gone soft."

Stella bit her lips together, holding back her chuckle. "Afraid it's going to ruin your reputation with the ladies?"

Liam turned his eyes back to the bed and let his head rest against the wall as a soft laugh crossed his lips. "There's no reputation with the ladies, nor do I care to have one."

"I don't know. It's a small town and you've been gone for a long time. It gives you an air of mystique."

When he spoke, his voice was deep and husky. "So, you think I'm mysterious?"

"Hardly." Stella did her best to ignore the tingles running through her core. "But who knows, it might help you out with the ladies in town."

"Good to know."

They sat in companionable silence as the soft sound of white noise filled the space around them. There, on the floor of his dimly lit bedroom, Stella struggled to remember why she was still so angry at Liam. Sure, he'd broken her heart all those years ago, but she'd moved on. She'd gotten over him, and built a life without him. A good life.

Keeping her eyes trained on the bed, she broke the silence. "I'm sorry I yelled at you this afternoon."

"It's not a big deal. Don't worry about it."

"It's just that my stress level was already through the roof with the party and then..." Stella let her words drift.

"Your mistress showed up in front of your boyfriend." Liam finished her sentence.

Cutting her eyes hard, Stella interjected quietly, "First of all, you're not my mistress. And second, Rick is not my boyfriend."

"You're right, I'm a guy. So does that make me your misteress or would it be your mister?" Liam arched a brow.

Stella jabbed her elbow at his side, barely making contact. "You know what I mean."

"Ouch. I didn't know you were the abusive type." Liam drew back like he was actually scared of her.

"I barely touched you." Stella rolled her eyes for emphasis.

There was a long pause before Liam spoke again. "On a serious note, what's the story with you and Rick? I mean, besides the fact that he's Willa's dad."

Stella's chest tightened at his words. She'd never had a problem explaining her relationship with Rick before, but suddenly, having to tell Liam made her nervous. Did he want to know because he was genuinely curious or because he was trying to size up the competition? Or worse, was he judging her for having a child out of wedlock?

"It's not a very exciting story." Stella took a deep breath and tried to calm her nerves. "We met at a bar in Charleston almost ten years ago. Willa was born nine months later, and we discovered we parent better as friends than a couple. The end."

"The end?" Liam turned and faced her full on, his eyes assessing her. "Oh no, you're not getting off that easy. The way he rested his hands on your shoulders, that's not a man who's just a friend. There's more to the story."

"You're wrong. There's nothing else to it, but even if there were, I don't kiss and tell." Stella's words came out curter than she intended.

"Fair enough." Liam nodded.

She expected him to push, to ask more questions, but instead he leaned back against the wall. What the hell did that mean? Was he mad because she wouldn't talk about her personal life? Was he respecting her space? She couldn't read him when he was so stoic.

"He's a dud." *Crap, why did you say that?*

Stella regretted the words the moment they crossed her lips. Her plan had been to use Rick as a barrier, and here she was telling the one man who got under her skin that Rick was no more than a friend who shared DNA with her daughter.

This was exactly what she was worried about. She couldn't be trusted alone in a room with Liam. She'd been here ten minutes and already she was suffering from word vomit.

"I didn't mean that. He's really kind and a great father to Willa," Stella stammered, trying to take back her admission.

"I didn't say anything." Liam gave her a lopsided grin.

"I was going through some stuff when Rick and I met. Let's just say it was a one-night stand that didn't work out quite as planned."

Her thoughts drifted back a decade. She'd been packing for a wedding convention in Charleston when she opened the local paper and saw the article about the Carefree boy who was doing big things in the

Rockies. She hadn't realized until that moment how much she'd been holding on to hope that Liam would come home. The news of him starting a business of his own had been the final crack in her heart.

Liam wasn't coming back.

For two days, her thoughts had drifted back to the article. Liam was out there living his life, and the only thing she'd done for two years was hold on to false hope that he'd see the error of his ways and come back to her.

Frustrated and heartbroken all over again, Stella had gone down to the lobby bar of her hotel. Her intention had been to simply drink away her sorrow, but then Rick had taken a seat beside her. She'd known from the moment he sat down he was as far from Liam as a man could be.

He was poised and sharply dressed in his three-piece suit, and when he opened his mouth she knew he was not an easy-going, fun-loving guy like her ex. He was intelligent, and a bit dry, but there was a sort of naive kindness to him that made her smile.

She didn't have a damn clue what the fundamental principles of physics and mathematics had to do with nuclear interactions and the transport of neutrons and gamma rays, but she'd listened as intently as one could in a half drunken state because it had absolutely nothing to do with Colorado or outdoor adventures.

Maybe it was all the wine consumed on an empty stomach but taking Rick back to her room had felt like a safe bet. He didn't exactly seem like the kind of man who had much success picking up women in hotel bars with all of his particle talk. It was just too bad the risk had outweighed the gamble.

Thankfully, Rick had been decent enough to exchange numbers with her the following morning. She'd made an assumption he was being polite and never intended to actually hear from her, but life hadn't turned out exactly how either one of them had planned.

Stella shoved the memories of the fateful night aside. Sitting on Liam's floor was not the time or place for a trip down memory lane. "So, what about you? Any ex-Mrs. Scott's running around the Rockies? Or maybe a potential Mrs. Scott?"

Stella held her breath as she waited for Liam to respond. It wasn't exactly the kind of information she wanted to know about her ex, but it felt like the logical response given they were already talking about partners.

"No, definitely no Mrs. Scott's running around the Rockies."

"No snow bunnies looking for private lessons?" Stella hid her nerves behind a soft laugh.

"Honestly, dating never seemed to make it up the priority list. I went on dates here and there, but there was always something else keeping my attention. I guess I never really thought the business would take off so fast, and then when it did, it was so time consuming I didn't have time to date. My business partner was the closest thing to a committed relationship I had, and that didn't exactly work out well."

"Were you two close?" Stella asked hesitantly, unsure if she should push the topic any further. She knew exactly how much heart and soul went into owning a company, and she could only imagine how devastated she'd be if anything ever happened to it.

"I thought we were." Liam rested his elbows on the tops of his knees and laced his fingers together. "I met Josh when I first moved out there. He was one of my first clients. I was doing some PT for him post rotator cuff surgery. We became friends and started hanging out. One night, we were at a bar downtown, and he started talking about this crazy idea he had to open his own excursion company. He'd been working ski patrol up on Breck for five years, but he wanted to do more than cart twisted ankles off the mountain."

"Anyway, he knew I had a minor in business administration and said we should partner up. He kept talking about how he had all these connections in the area, but I had the brains to run the operation. It took us almost two years to pull it all together, but we finally opened up shop in this tiny shack of a building." Liam let out a genuine laugh.

"What's so funny?" Stella was confused by the sudden change in his demeanor.

"I haven't thought about the beginning in years. We were just these two crazy kids with a big dream, and not a pot to piss in. I don't even know how the hell we pulled it off, but things took off. Josh was right about his connections. He had people lined up from the moment we opened the doors. Word spread and the next thing I knew, we were five years in with forty-three employees and an apparel line."

"That's amazing. You should be proud of your success."

Liam was quiet for a long moment. "I am. I guess I just hate the way it all ended. It's like you have this idea of where you're headed and then out of nowhere life takes a hard right turn, you know?"

Boy did she ever know. Her life was like a West Virginia mountain road. The only thing that seemed to have worked out the way she planned was Pebble Creek. As for the rest of it, she'd never seen it coming. "I think I know what you mean."

Cast in the dim light of the lamp, Stella stared deep into his emerald eyes as the years melted away. He wasn't the same Liam she'd known years ago. The man sitting before her now was passionate and deep. The kind of man who cared about the world around him. The kind of man who babysat his sister's newborn so she could sleep.

Stella's heart beat against her chest with an urgency she hadn't felt in far too long, as old feelings bubbled their way back to the surface.

"Can I tell you something?" Liam's words were soft, but his tone was intense. Deep and husky.

Instinctively, Stella leaned in. Her eyes drawn to his smooth lips. "Mmm hmm."

"When I took the job in Colorado…" Liam hesitated, and she could have sworn he leaned closer, too. "I never wanted to leave you behind. I wanted you to come with me."

Chapter Eleven

Liam's chest tightened as he waited for Stella to process his words. He hadn't planned to blurt it out that way—hell, he hadn't planned to bring it up at all—but something deep inside of him needed her to know. No matter what the future held, he needed Stella to know his decision to leave had never been about her.

"Say something." Liam let his hand rest gently on top of hers.

"I should go."

"Say something different." His heart clenched tighter as she pulled her hand back and began to stand. Not ready for the conversation to be over, Liam stood and gently grabbed her forearm before she could walk away. "Stella, wait. Let me explain."

For once in his life, she actually listened.

Shocked, Liam took in her motionless body. Her green eyes were locked on his. The soft curve of her shoulders was now stiff and rigid. The tension rolled off of her in waves.

Shit. He had her attention and absolutely no idea what to do with it. There was no plan. No grand apology for being an ass all those years ago, only a driving need to have her back in his life.

Releasing the light hold on her arm, Liam scrubbed a hand through his hair. "I'm not really sure where to start."

If looks could kill, he'd be a corpse six-feet under. "I don't know, Liam, how about the part where you took a job halfway across the country and forgot to mention it to your fiancé. Or, better yet, the part where you walked out on me and never looked back. I guess it's true what they say, girls pick men like their fathers. He just had the decency to never come back."

Once, very early in their relationship, Liam had asked about Stella's parents. She'd made it clear at the time it was just she and her mom, and the subject wasn't up for discussion. Liam had never pressed the issue. At the time, it hadn't seemed important.

Clearly, he'd been wrong.

"Stella, I…" What did he say to that? She wasn't wrong. He'd left Carefree and never reached out. When he'd come home to visit, he'd intentionally stayed in his own town and never headed near Pebble Creek. He'd been careful to avoid any of the places they'd frequented.

As the years passed, the trips back to South Carolina became fewer and farther between, but somehow the memory of Stella stayed with him. It was the little things that got him the most. The scent of her perfume on a stranger as they passed by. Her favorite song on the radio. But what haunted him the most was the flashes of auburn hair in a crowd. How many times had he thought it was her?

Stella closed her eyes and let out a heavy sigh before glancing back up at him. "Look, I understand what you're trying to do, but this isn't necessary. We broke up twelve years ago. I've moved on. You've moved on. Life moves on."

Before he could process his own thoughts, Liam lifted his hands and pressed them along her jaw line. Pulling her in, he kissed her like it was his dying wish. For the briefest moment, he let himself get lost in the woman he'd loved for so long.

The sudden weight of her hands wrapped around his wrists felt like shackles as she pulled back. Opening his eyes, Liam stared at the sadness swirling in her pale green eyes.

What did you do? "Stel—"

"No." Releasing his wrists, she took a hesitant step back. "You can't go around kissing people and expecting them to forget the past."

Raw emotion gripped his chest. God, this woman frustrated him more than anything in his entire life. He wanted to yell at her. Tell her how wrong and stubborn she was being. He'd seen the way she was looking at him earlier, her eyes trained on his lips. He was certain he wasn't the only one who wanted to explore this thing between them.

"Hello?" Liam and Stella turned in unison toward the bedroom door in time to see Kat's face appear in the opening. "Oh, hey Stella."

"Shh…you're going to wake up your demon possessed child," Liam whispered while casting a quick glance at his sleeping niece. "What are you doing here?"

A sinister smiled twisted the corner of Kat's lips. "I could ask you the same thing."

Confused and annoyed for the interruption, Liam shot her a questioning look. "What are you talking about? I live here."

"Oh, I meant more like what's happening here?" Kat swirled her finger in tiny circles in their direction. "Because it looks a lot like you're using my newborn to pick up chicks."

"Kat!" He'd never wanted to murder his sister so much in his life.

He was on thin ice with Stella and the last thing he needed was Kat chipping away at the surface with a pick axe.

"I was actually leaving." Stella moved to the bed and grabbed her belongings before walking back to the bedroom door. "She's very precious. Congratulations."

"Thank you." Kat's face beamed with pride.

"Well, goodnight." Stella lifted her hand in a slight wave as she disappeared through the door.

Everything was happening so fast and yet, somehow, his body was stuck in slow motion. He wanted to beg her to stop, to let him explain, but for the life of him, Liam couldn't find his words or make his feet move. Like some out of body experience, all he could do was watch his night fall apart before his eyes.

"Are you having a stroke?" Kat's voice filled the quiet space.

The sound of the storm door closing pulled him from his trance. Turning his attention to his sister, Liam's anger flared. "You have impeccable timing."

"And you really know how to win them back." Kat spoke softly as she leaned down to pick up her daughter who'd begun to stir.

"I don't even want to know how much you heard." Liam let out a heavy sigh. His sister loved gossip and juicy details. There was no doubt he'd be hearing about this until the end of time.

"Enough to get that you suck at apologies. So, why are you still standing here? Go get your girl."

*****

The cool night air was a welcome relief against Stella's heated cheeks. Hurrying down the exterior steps, she dug through her purse frantically in search of her keys.

It was all too much to process. Liam's closeness. His words.

The man she'd spent so many years resenting, blaming for all the wrong in her life, was gone. The man she saw tonight was honest and vulnerable. A man who wasn't afraid to take accountability and apologize. A man nothing like her father.

He was exactly the man she'd always wanted him to be and that scared her more than anything.

"Shit." Stella cursed the jagged strips of metal hiding in the depths of her bag. "Where the hell are my keys?"

This couldn't be happening.

Not now.

How many nights had she laid in bed, wishing he would come back? Wishing he would change his mind and want her too. And now here he was, the exact man she'd wished for, but she wasn't that same young girl. She had a daughter to think about. A business to run. The last thing she needed was to want a man who'd caused her so much pain.

And boy, did she want him.

No, what she wanted was time to think. Space to clear her head. Hell, maybe to scream into the abyss at how sucky life's timing was.

"Jackpot." A wave of relief washed over her the moment her fingers wrapped around the metal key ring.

"Stella, stop."

Spinning on her heels, she was stunned to see Liam towering over her. She'd been so lost in her own head she hadn't heard him coming across the yard.

"You're wrong." His words washed over her.

"I'm not doing this right now, Liam." She tried to sound firm, but her words came out weak. Like her own little kryptonite, she was helpless when it came to him. Staying mad was easy from a distance, but in his presence, she was a pile of mush.

"I never got over you. It's why I never settled down. No one was ever you."

She could practically feel the sincerity dripping from his words.

Shit! She definitely didn't need to do this right now. Turning her back to him, Stella hurried her way across the lawn to where her car was parked on the street.

"I know things aren't the same, but I don't think you got over me either," Liam continued.

His words slithered up her spine like a serpent. Stella stopped next to the driver's side door and faced him head on. "You don't know anything about my life for the last decade."

"I know if you hated me as much as you try to pretend, you wouldn't have slept with me last weekend."

"I was drunk. People do stupid things when they drink." She countered.

"Not you. And you weren't that drunk."

"You don't know what I was."

"Are you drunk tonight?" The corner of his mouth twisted up ever so slightly.

"What? Of course not." She wanted to smack him for even insinuating she came here drunk. And what a stupid question. It was obvious she hadn't been drinking. "Trust me, my head is very clear right now."

"Very clear?" He questioned her sentiment.

"Very."

"Are you sure about that?" Liam took a step closer, crowding her space.

"I'm beginning to think you're the one who's been drinking since you keep asking the same damn question." She was trying hard to keep her frustration in place, but the heat coursing through her veins suddenly had nothing to do with anger and everything to do with his closeness. "There's absolutely nothing impeding my ability to think clearly tonight."

The last part was an outright lie, but he didn't need to know that.

His body inched closer. "Then tell me you didn't enjoy it just as much as I did."

"I already told you I was drunk." She was losing her steam. Fast.

"That's not what I said. Tell me you haven't imagined it a million times from the moment you took on Miles and Julia as clients." His husky words rippled across her skin.

Her heart raced, pounding against her chest. "You've lost your mind."

"Have I?" Liam closed the small space between them and rested his hand on her car before lowering his lips to her ear. "Tell me you haven't been thinking about it all night."

Closing her eyes, Stella breathed in the scent of him. "Not at all."

"Not even once?" His breath tickled the skin beneath her ear lobe.

"Nope." Her words were weak, but her resolve was weaker. Shifting her stance, she felt his growing erection against her hip.

"So, this is all in my head?" He whispered along her jaw line as he moved his face in front of hers.

"Mmm hmm."

His hand dropped from her car as he took a small step back. "Fair enough."

The sensible part of her knew they should talk about the bomb he'd dropped, but they'd waited twelve years to have that conversation, what was one more night? If she was going off the deep end, she might as well go head first.

Sliding her fingers into his belt loop, Stella stopped him from moving any further away. "Where are you going?"

A low chuckle rumbled through his chest. "I don't think you want to know the answer to that."

"And why wouldn't I want to know?" Her mind raced trying to decipher the meaning behind his words.

"Don't look so concerned." Liam reached around the hold she had on his belt loops and adjusted himself. "Just a little personal business I need to take care of."

Her eyes followed his movements. "Oh!"

"Unless you've changed your mind and want to help?"

Her hormones overthrew her good sense. "I'm kind of good at personal business."

In a flurry of motion, Liam unhooked her fingers from their hold on his jeans and swept his left arm behind her knees as he hoisted her into his arms.

Startled, Stella let out a high-pitched shriek. "What are you doing?"

"Taking you back inside my apartment before you can change your mind."

Stella wiggled her legs, trying to free herself from his hold. "I can walk, you know."

"Hell no, not gonna happen. You might change your mind and run." Liam tightened his grip and started across the yard.

"What about your sister and niece?"

"Kat followed me out and went back to her house. The apartment's empty." Liam marched across the yard, full steam ahead.

It was crazy and foolish, but being wrapped in his arms was the best feeling she'd felt in a long time. As they reached the bottom of the steps, he lowered her to the first plank. Back on her feet, Stella turned to face him. "What? No Tarzan carrying me up the steps?"

"At risk of this coming out completely wrong, I'm not that in shape. I spent the last few months in an office, not on the side of a mountain."

Stella laughed. The man looked like he hadn't missed a day at the gym. "Don't lie, you want to watch my ass walking up the steps."

Liam shrugged. "You're not wrong. It's a fantastic ass."

"You're such a man." Shaking her head, Stella turned to head up the steps when Liam's hand locked on to hers. Turning back, she shot him a questioning look. "Change your mind already?"

"No, I'm trying to decide if this is real." Stella watched the hesitation tug at his brow before he continued. "Are you sure this is what you want, Stella?"

Liam was right about a lot of things. She'd spent every day of the past four months wondering what it would be like to see him again. Because as much as her life had moved on, a part of her never let go. The large piece of her heart she'd given so many years ago still belonged to him.

Wrapping her arms around Liam's shoulders, Stella pulled him close until only a breath could fit between their lips. "I never got over you either."

Chapter Twelve

Liam couldn't believe the scene unfolding before him. Less than eight hours ago, Stella had told him in no uncertain terms there was no room for him in her life, and now here he was watching her hips sway as she made her way back up to his apartment.

It was a ballsy move pushing her the way he had, but hell, maybe actions did speak louder than words. If a little suggestive motion was all it took, he'd keep his damn mouth shut and let his body do all the talking. Whatever it took to get her in his bed.

Stepping back through his front door, Liam stopped long enough to switch the deadbolt to lock before looking up to see two beautiful green eyes staring him down.

"Afraid I might run away?" Stella taunted him from the middle of his living room, her arms crossed in front of her chest.

"More afraid my nosy-ass sister will make a reappearance." With that thought in mind, Liam moved to the window next and let down the blinds.

"Can never be too careful."

The sweet sound of her laughter filled his soul.

"You have no idea." Liam shook his head at the truth in his words. "Now, about this business you're good at…"

He watched the blush bloom across her cheeks and spread down her neck to her chest as he started across the room. The slight shift in her hips made him wonder if it was nerves or anticipation she was wrestling with, but either way she was standing her ground.

"Right, your personal business." A nervous laughter escaped across her lips.

Moving in close, Liam trailed his fingers across her right forearm before giving it a light tug, effectively uncrossing her arms in one swift movement. With her body opened up to him, he took in the sight before him.

She was beautiful, every square inch of her.

For the first time since he'd come home, Liam drank in the sight of her. No longer did he have to watch her from a distance or cast quick glances in hopes she wouldn't catch him. Taking advantage of the opportunity, he let his eyes linger across her body. She had matured in every perfect way possible.

Stella lifted her arms and wrapped them around his neck, cutting off his view. "Didn't anyone teach you it's impolite to stare?"

She was definitely nervous. He may have been forward down on the street, but he needed to take this slow. Not that he minded taking such things nice and slow. "Business one-oh-one, never miss an opportunity when she presents herself."

"She?" Stella cocked her head slightly. "I must have missed that lecture."

Liam slipped his arms around her waist and pulled her closer. He loved the feel of her body pressed against his. Like it was made to fit perfectly in his grasp. "Intro to Personal Business. I believe they only offered it to those minoring in business. We didn't get the fancy *I'm-a-serious-business-major* classes."

Her soft chuckle vibrated against his chest. "You're ridiculous."

"Hey, I take personal business very serious." As Liam shrugged, the lift of his shoulders pulled Stella closer, leaving only a breath between them.

Unable to resist her closeness any longer, he tilted his head down and brushed his mouth against her smooth lips. Her soft moan was music to his ears. Swiping his tongue against the thin crease, her lips parted, and he deepened the kiss as the tension from the past week melted away.

With Stella wrapped in his arms, their mouths pressed firmly against one another, he felt like he was twenty-three again. Passion moved through them in waves, pulling him further under her spell. There wasn't anything he wouldn't do to keep her here, pressed against his body.

Moving slowly, Liam let his hands drift over the small curve of her back and down to the fantastic ass he'd happily watched climb the steps to his apartment. His gentle squeeze pressed her firmly against his growing erection, earning him another moan.

It quickly became a game, seeing which movements would elicit the sweet sound of her pleasure echoing in her chest. Breaking the connection, Liam worked his way across her jaw line and began pressing kisses down the side of her throat. Encouraged by the sharp intake of breath and her fingers locked in his hair, he shifted his hands down to her thighs. Before she could protest, he lifted her legs and wrapped them around his waist.

There was no argument this time as he carried her across the room and into the bedroom where they'd spent most of the evening. Only now, there would be no hushed voices. If he had anything to say about it, there would be plenty of noise filling the room.

Lowering Stella to the bed, Liam made quick work of discarding his t-shirt. Pulling it over his head, he let the cotton drop to the floor at his feet. The look of satisfaction on her face would fuel his fantasies for weeks to come.

*****

Stella stared up at the beautiful man towering over her. His body was a piece of art. Muscle chiseled into hard stone. Tan, smooth skin flowed down his torso and curved into a hard V that dipped below his belt, pointing to the promise of something extraordinary.

Inhaling deep, she tried to steady her frazzled nerves. She wanted him, there was no denying it, but this time meant so much more than their night in the boat house. She needed him more than the air in her lungs, and yet, she knew taking this step would unequivocally change their future.

Closing her eyes, heat boiled in her core and swept across her skin like an inferno. Every inch of her was on fire, burning for the man she'd loved for so long.

"We don't have to do this." Liam's deep voice brushed across her cheek as his fingers slipped through her hair.

The simple way he caressed her head eased her worry. Lifting her gaze, she stared into his worried eyes. "No, I want to."

Before she lost her nerve again, Stella lifted her fingers to his buckle and pulled the leather strap loose from the belt loop. With the belt out of the way, she made quick work releasing the button on his denim jeans. She'd barely begun lowering the zipper when his strong hands clasped around hers.

"That can wait." Lifting her hands, Liam bent and pressed a gentle kiss to her knuckles. "I have other things in mind first."

One minute, Stella was sitting on the side of the bed, and the next Liam's hands were beneath her thighs hoisting her toward the middle of the bed. Before she could utter a protest, he was hovering over, his heated eyes staring straight into her soul.

And then his lips were on her.

He was everywhere at once, his lips burning a trail of hot kisses down her throat, as his hands moved up her torso. Arching her back, she pressed into him as his lips marched across her collarbone and down her sternum. Lost in the wonder of his mouth against her skin, she was barely aware of her cotton blouse slipping up her ribs until hands moved across her tender breasts.

"Lift your head," he commanded in a sultry voice.

Doing as he asked, Stella lifted slightly and raised her arms above her head as he slipped the fabric over her hair. Before she could pull her arms free of the shirt, Liam locked a strong hand around her wrists and placed them back on the bed above her head. With a sinister smile, he twisted the fabric tight and tucked it into what she could only assume was a makeshift knot.

"Leave your hands there." He commanded again in the same deep, sultry voice.

The sharp intake of air was her only answer.

Stella fought the urge to wriggle free. She wasn't one to be told what to do, but something in his commands turned her desire up to burning hell.

Softly, he trailed a finger down the outside of her arm and around the bottom curve of her shoulder, before slipping his hand beneath her back. In one quick movement, he unclasped her bra.

Pulling back, Liam placed his hands along her ribs and slowly began his ascent back up her torso, taking her bra with them in the same way he'd removed her shirt. Only this time, his fingers stopped briefly when he reached her nipples, pinching the tender skin between his thumb and forefinger. The pressure was just enough to cause a delicious sting to radiate across her breast.

With her bra stowed by her wrists, she watched as Liam shifted on the bed. He was headed south this time. Her core muscles clenched tight as dampness pooled between her legs.

He was less delicate as he released the button and zipper of her jeans. "Lift your hips, sweetheart."

Obliging, her anticipation grew as he tugged her underwear down with the denim. Just as with her shirt, Liam left her clothing bunched around her ankles.

"Liam." She breathed his name.

A sly smile crossed his lips as he glanced back up her naked body. "Shhh...it'll be worth it, baby girl. Just wait and see."

This was it.

This was how she would die.

Consumed by the flame of her own desire.

*****

Stella woke to the morning sun and a delicious ache in her muscles. Stretching, the tightness radiated from her shoulders down to her toes. It had been a long time since her body experienced that kind of workout in one night. Strike that, she'd never experienced anything like what Liam had done to her.

Ever.

"Good morning, beautiful." His smooth voice crept across her bare shoulder. "Or should I say, good afternoon?"

"What?" Flinging herself upright in the bed, Stella searched the room for a clock. "What time is it?"

Liam chuckled as he ran a finger down her spine. "Almost eleven."

"Holy crap!" Jumping up from the bed, she frantically searched for her clothes that had been slung about the room in their moment of passion. Her bra and blouse were the first to appear in a heap beside the bed. With quick work, she slipped them on before noticing her underwear hanging from the nob on his nightstand. Grabbing the silky cotton, she hurried them up her thighs. As she glanced around for her jeans, her eyes locked on Liam lying back against the headboard, his hands tucked behind his head with a lop-sided smile spreading from ear to ear. "What's so funny?"

"I'm just wondering if I should pencil in *Stella storming out* on my calendar for next Sunday? Seems there might be a habit forming."

Regret tightened in her chest. He wasn't wrong, though technically he'd been the one to leave first last weekend, but only because she'd shown him the door. If he hadn't woken, she would have snuck out without a word. "You're funny, it's just that…"

It occurred to her, she hadn't thought about how any of this affected her daughter. She'd been so caught up in the moment, making hasty confessions of old feelings, that she never once thought about what it meant to bring a man into Willa's life.

"It's just what?" Liam sat up on the bed, a look of concern replacing his playful smile.

"I have a daughter." The words rushed across her lips.

A new realization dawned. They had never discussed kids during their engagement. Maybe it was foolish and naive on her part—not that it mattered since they never made it down the aisle—but she'd made a natural assumption they'd have kids after they got married. Had he even wanted to have kids? Would it have been another massive pothole in their relationship when she discovered he didn't want any of his own?

"I'm fully aware." Liam's brows scrunched.

Clearly, he didn't understand what she was saying. "No, I mean I have a daughter. As in, for a lack of a better word, I come with baggage. I'm not the same girl I was in my twenties that can run off into the sunset with you. I have responsibilities. I have to think about Willa. And she has a father who is very much present in her life."

She waited for Liam to process her words. Being with her meant taking on a nine-year-old and another man. Not that she and Rick had a real relationship outside of co-parenting, but he would always be a part of her life. Could Liam handle having another man in the picture?

She watched in awkward anticipation as Liam removed the covers and slipped from the edge of the bed. He moved silently as he grabbed his jeans from the floor and slipped them back up around his waist. This was it. The moment he realized she was too much to take on.

Closing her eyes, Stella let the memories of their night drift through her mind like a montage. She would cherish their amazing—yet brief—time together. In an odd way, at least this time there was closure. Maybe knowing the truth about their past was all she needed to finally let go.

"Stel, open your eyes."

Following his instructions, Stella opened her eyes to find him standing right in front of her. He was a sight for sore eyes, with his bare chest and rumpled hair. She would hold on to this image for a long time. If only she could capture it on her phone so she could pull look at it from time to time.

She stood motionless as Liam lifted his hands and placed them on either side of her face, cradling her in his palms.

This was their goodbye.

"I know you have a daughter. She's pretty fantastic from what I've seen. And I get that Rick is in her life, as he should be, but…"

Oh God, here it was, the *but*.

"…none of that matters. I mean, of course it matters. I guess what I'm saying is I never expected your life to be exactly how it was when I left. If it were, well, I'd kind of feel sorry for you. We grew up and maybe our lives took different paths, but who cares. The important thing is those paths led us back to one another."

Overwhelmed with more emotion than she could handle without caffeine, Stella blurted the first thing that came to mind. "I have to eat pizza."

Liam's laughter filled the room. "I don't know what the hell that has to do with the price of tea in China, but okay, we can eat pizza."

Stella shook her head, trying to form a coherent thought. "No, I mean, that's the thing. I promised Willa I would pick her up in time for Sunday pizza. It's kind of our thing we do…usually after church."

"Oh, I see. Well, you should probably get going."

The words were out of her mouth before she could process what she was doing. "Do you want to come with us?"

Chapter Thirteen

"Why aren't we ordering?"

Stella glanced up from her wrist to see her daughter's curious eyes locked on her. Since the moment she'd stepped out of Liam's apartment, she'd debated how to broach the subject with Willa, but she was out of time. "I invited Liam to join us for lunch. He's been helping out around the office, and I thought it would be a nice way to say thank you. Is that okay with you?" Stella tried to keep her voice indifferent.

A task that would be easier if she hadn't spent all night living out every fantasy she'd ever had.

Willa smiled from across the table. "It's fine with me...as long as he doesn't eat all the cheese pizza."

"We can order extra today." Stella returned her daughter's smile. "I'm sure Liam will want his own. I doubt he'll want your cheese or my veggie pizza. He seems more like a meat kind of guy, don't you think?"

"I bet he likes pepperonis. Maybe even sausage or bacon. That's a guy's pizza."

"Sounds like a guy's pizza to me." Stella glanced at the door. It was twelve twenty-nine and still no sign of Liam.

Her stomach twisted into a tight knot, the same way it did before every wedding when the anticipation and doubt took over. The only difference between then and now was the fact that her emotions felt like they'd been dragged across sandpaper. Add to it the exhaustion thanks to the vigorous workout the night before, and she might as well be the conductor of the Hot Mess Express.

Turning back to her daughter, Stella did her best to push aside all the raw emotions she was feeling. "What do you say we go ahead and order ours?"

"Sure." Willa shrugged as she fiddled with the shakers on the table. "I am kind of starving."

As Stella stood from her chair, the door to the restaurant opened and Liam appeared. Her breath caught in her throat as the man wreaking havoc on her soul approached. He was dressed in a pair of cargo shorts and a black Mile High Excursions hoodie. It was the first time she'd seen him wear any of his company's apparel, and damn if it didn't look good on him. Or maybe it was the rugged five o'clock shadow that made him look so delicious.

"Ladies," Liam called as he approached the table.

"Hey, Liam." Willa spun in her seat. "What's behind your back?"

Stella had been so focused on the man that she hadn't realized he was holding something. Slowly, Liam swung his arm in front of him and produced a long slender box wrapped in what looked like paper towels.

"I didn't have any wrapping paper." Liam handed the package to Willa who was beaming from ear to ear.

"You got me a present?" Willa took the package from his hand.

"It's still your birthday weekend, right?"

"It is!" Without hesitation, Willa began ripping at the paper. "Mom, Liam got me a kite!"

"I see, sweetie." A small shred of relief washed over Stella when she realized the present was for her daughter and not herself. The thought of having to explain why Liam had shown up with a present made her anxiety crackle.

Liam smiled. "I wasn't sure which one you would like best, but I thought the dragonfly looked pretty cool."

"Can we go to the waterfront park after lunch to fly it?" Willa glanced between Stella and Liam.

"Well, that's up to your mom."

"Can we, Mom?"

Both sets of eyes locked on Stella. "Sure. It seems like there's a good breeze coming in off the water."

Jumping up from her seat, Willa wrapped her arms around Liam's waist. "Thank you, Liam from Colorado."

Liam scrubbed a hand through her hair. "I'm glad you like it, kid."

Stella's heart wrenched at the sight of her daughter's arms wrapped around the man who'd once held her with all the love in the world.

Lifting her head, Stella's eyes locked on the two emerald pools staring back at her. "I was going to go order at the counter if you'd like to join me?" She lifted her hand and gestured toward the counter.

"Sounds like a plan." Liam released his hold on her daughter.

With Willa seated back at the table, Stella made her way to the register to place their order. As she moved through the sea of tables, she could feel Liam's eyes watching her every move.

Stepping in line, Stella turned back to check on Willa and nearly plowed into Liam's chest. "Oh!"

"Hi." Mischief swirled in his beautiful green eyes.

"Stop, you can't do that." Stella spun toward the menu hanging above the register and studied it like her life depended on it.

Liam's smooth voice crept over her shoulder. "I can't do what exactly?"

Glancing back, Stella whispered, "Look at me with those *I've seen you naked* eyes."

Liam's laughter drifted over her body. She could feel the heat rolling off him in waves. "All I said was hi."

"Yes, but it's the way you said it." Stella fought the blush threatening to creep across her skin.

"And how exactly did I say it?"

"Like you're auditioning for a romantic comedy."

"Well..." Liam cocked a brow.

"Next." A teenage boy called from behind the counter.

Glad to have the distraction, Stella stepped up to the counter and placed her order, before sliding out of the way for Liam to order. As they turned to head back to the table, she placed a gentle hand on his arm and pulled him to the side. "Look, we did a lot of *things* last night—"

"Things?" Liam laughed, interrupting her before she could finish her thought.

"Yes, *things!* But I have to take this slow with Willa. It's one thing to make suggestive comments to me, but you can't do that around her. I don't want her getting the wrong idea. She gets attached easily, and I don't want her to get hurt in all this." Stella waved a hand between them.

Their night had been magical, but in the light of day, there was a part of her that was hesitant to trust him. She had to be smart about this. For her heart and for her daughter's sake.

"Stella, I'm not a fool. I would never be disrespectful or inappropriate in front of your daughter. I hope you know that?"

"I just needed to say it out loud. Protecting her is my sole priority." Stella glanced across the room to where Willa sat examining the kite Liam had bought her.

"As it should be." The playfulness was gone from his voice. "I know you asked me to keep my distance, and I will respect that, but I felt bad for not bringing a gift to her party yesterday. I hope it's not a problem that I got her something?"

Stella took in the sincerity in his eyes. "It's fine. You didn't need to feel bad about it, but it's very sweet of you to bring her a gift." This wasn't the time or place to get into a heavy conversation. Needing to lighten the mood before they sat down, Stella smiled up at Liam. "As for the wrapping job, now that you should feel bad about."

"Wow, way to go straight for the jugular." Liam feigned a look of shock. "On that note, I'm going to sit with the kid. At least she's nice to me."

"Hey, I'm buying you pizza," Stella joked as she followed Liam back to their table.

"Yeah, and at this rate, you're going to have to buy me apology ice cream too."

"What's apology ice cream?" Willa questioned as both Liam and Stella took their seats.

Before she could come up with a reasonable explanation, Liam let out a soft laugh. "It's what your mom is going to have to buy me for making fun of my wrapping paper."

*****

Liam watched as the colorful dragonfly soared against the clear blue sky. Other than a touchy moment with Stella while in line, lunch had gone off without a hitch. Willa had been more than happy to fill any silent voids with chatter about school and her friends. The more time he spent around the girl, the more impressed he was by her intelligence. He'd known from their first conversation in the diner that she was pretty smart where math was concerned, but it seemed she was excelling at all subjects.

"Look how high it is, Liam." Willa's sweet voice drifted across the grass.

"I see. You're doing great." He smiled and gave her a thumbs up.

With the open space and the breeze coming off the sound, the park was a perfect place to fly a kite. How many times had he come here with his father and done the same exact thing as a kid?

Glancing over at Stella, Liam thought about what life would have been like if he hadn't gone to Colorado. It was easy to envision a life with Stella and a few kids running around now, but life wasn't some computer file he could copy and paste himself into. He hadn't been ready for this life twelve years ago, but looking at it now, he longed for a family of his own.

Sure, he could have stayed and married Stella all those years ago, but the truth was, he wasn't sure they would have survived the growing pains of early adulthood. He'd needed Colorado. Needed the time to grow up. Needed to experience life. If he'd stayed, there was a good chance he would have ended up resenting her, and where would that have left them?

"You're good with kids." Stella smiled as he approached the park bench and took a seat next to her.

"I don't know about that, she's pretty easy to be around. I think it helps that we're on the same level."

Stella's lips turned up into a grin. "Are you saying she has the maturity of a thirty-five-year-old man, or you have the maturity of a nine-year-old girl?"

"Definitely the latter." Liam let out a soft laugh. "Did you ever think about having more kids?"

The question was out of his mouth before he realized it. The last thing he wanted to do was stir up any awkwardness. The worrisome look on her face said it all. Had she assumed he was referring to them having kids?

Desperate to keep the conversation from completely derailing, Liam trained his eyes on Willa. "Just curious if you and Rick had ever thought about a baby brother or sister for Willa."

He hated the thought of even bringing Slick Rick's name into their conversation, but it was the first excuse that came to mind.

Stella was quiet for a long moment. "When Willa came along, I was shocked to say the least. I'm pretty sure Rick never intended to hear from me, much less with news he was going to be a father, but he handled it well. Better than I expected. He's a wonderful father, but I knew from the beginning there would never be more between us. Definitely not more children. I don't know that I could have handled five like your mom, but I used to think two or three would be nice. Guess life had a different plan."

A fact she undoubtedly blamed on him. Liam did his best to keep his tone light and playful. "Says the only child. Try growing up with four annoying siblings, you'd probably think differently."

"Did you ever think about having kids?"

Her question surprised him. As much as it felt like a normal conversation between two adults, he sensed there was more to her question. "I don't know, I always assumed I would have kids, but I guess the opportunity never really presented itself. Seems kind of a moot point now."

"Why do you say that?" Stella's brow scrunched like she didn't understand his words.

He wanted to point out the obvious. The only thing he was interested in was her, and she'd all but said she wasn't having any more kids. Not to mention, one night with his niece had about done him in.

"For starters, it's not like I'm getting any younger."

"You could always find a younger woman who still has time to pop a few out."

The way she said it, so blasé, threw him. What the hell was going on? Had he completely misinterpreted the night before, because he thought they were on the same page. Hell, she'd invited him to lunch with her daughter. Sure, she'd freaked out a little this morning, and again at the restaurant, but working through a few kinks was bound to happen. This, however, felt like she was pushing him away. "Stella, what's going on?"

So much for keeping things awkward-free.

"Nothing's going on. I'm just saying you could still have a family if that's what you want." He wasn't buying the gentle smile curving her lips.

Acutely aware of Willa's presence not far in the open grass, Liam lowered his voice. "The only thing I want is you. I thought I made that pretty damn clear last night."

Stella seemed to have the same thought as she glanced over to her daughter. Lowering her voice to match his, she didn't bother to look at him when she continued. "All I'm saying is that I wouldn't blame you if you wanted something more. Something of your own. I come as a package deal and that's not for everyone."

Every fiber of his being wanted to show her just how much he wanted her, but wrapping Stella in his arms wouldn't help anything. She wanted to take things slow with Willa and he respected that, but this sudden doubt was killing him. Running a hand through his hair, Liam searched for the words that would make her believe him.

"Stel, look at me." Liam waited for her to turn toward him. "You have a daughter, I know that. I knew that last night. If you think that bothers me, you're wrong."

"It's more than Willa. Rick is in our lives too. You can say that doesn't bother you now, but a few months from now, you might not feel the same way."

And there it was. She was afraid he was going to change his mind again.

He wanted to punch the twenty-three-year-old-version of himself in the nuts for not handling the situation better back then. He'd sown a seed of doubt so deep, she couldn't trust his words now. There was a part of him that couldn't blame her for not trusting him. He'd made promises before, and in her eyes, he'd broken them so easily. The other part of him wanted nothing more than to let the past go and move forward.

"I can't change the past, and although part of me wishes I could, I wouldn't. Even if I had a genie in my pocket. Because changing the past would mean taking away that amazing little girl. All I'm asking is that you give us a chance. A real chance. We had a good thing going before and I know that was a long time ago, and I get things are different, but I think we could have a good thing again."

"Liam, I—"

"Come to dinner at my parents' house tonight." Liam cut off her words before she could say something else discouraging. "They still do Sunday dinner with the whole gang. You can get reacquainted with everyone, and they can meet Willa. It will be fun. I'm sure my brothers will be happy to bring up every embarrassing moment of my life." He didn't want to push too hard, but he needed to remind her how amazing they were together. He needed her to see she fit perfectly in his world.

"I don't know. It's a lot to spring on Willa."

"What's a lot?" They both glanced up in unison to find Willa standing a few feet away.

He'd been so caught up in trying to talk Stella off the ledge that he hadn't noticed Willa moving closer to them. "I was inviting you and your mom to dinner at my parents' house tonight."

It was a risky move that was likely going to land him in the doghouse, but he needed the kid on his side. If he could just get her there, Stella would remember how much she used to love his family.

148

"Can we go, Mom?"

"Yeah mom, can you?" Liam shot her an apologetic smile.

Stella lifted her finger and swayed it back and forth between he and Willa. "I'm on to you two."

It wasn't the end of the conversation, he knew that, but at least Stella hadn't stormed off or told him to go to hell.

Chapter Fourteen

Stella stepped through the Scott's front door just as nervous as the first time she'd visited their home. Aside from some updated photos on the wall, the place hadn't changed a bit in the last decade. It was as though she had been transported right back into her past.

Next to her, Willa pressed into her side as her daughter's small hand wrapped around her forearm. "We don't have to stay if you don't want to." Stella glanced down to reassure her daughter. "Liam's family will understand if you want to go."

Willa's voice was quiet as she tugged on Stella's arm. "It's not that. I really have to pee."

"Oh." Stella shot Liam an apologetic smile. "Will you excuse us for a moment?"

"Absolutely, I'll be out back with everyone." Liam scrubbed a hand through Willa's hair. A gesture that did little to ease Stella's nerves.

She was putting on a good face for her daughter's sake, but the truth of the matter was she felt anything but comfortable. Stella wanted to believe Liam's words in the park, but she couldn't escape the nagging feeling that she was going to end up on the hurt end of whatever this was they were doing.

It was one thing to get lost in the fantasy of life when it was just the two of them in his bed, but reality had a way of crashing the party. Maybe some would consider it jumping the gun to think so far in the future, but she couldn't risk letting herself go down the rabbit hole only to find out a few months in that Liam wanted things she couldn't give him.

She was neck deep in raising a daughter and running a business. There was no time to start over with a new family. Just the thought of trudging through sleepless nights again made her spine curl. Pebble Creek was too demanding to try and split her focus between work and a newborn. Her diaper days were well behind her.

Pushing the thought aside, Stella smiled down at her daughter and pointed down the hall. "The bathroom's this way."

As they stepped inside, Stella closed the door and turned to find her daughter giving her a curious look. "How do you know where the bathroom is?"

Right, as far as Willa knew, Liam was an old friend. Her daughter was completely unaware of how many times she'd been to this house in her early twenties.

"Well." Stella started slowly, choosing her words carefully. "Once upon a very long time ago, I used to come here with Liam to visit his parents."

"Why?" Willa asked from her perch on the toilet.

There was no surprise the vague answer was not satisfying enough for her curious daughter, but it had been worth a shot. Not to mention, there was a really good chance the topic of their past relationship was going to come up, so it was best to get any shock over now. "Because Liam and I used to be boyfriend and girlfriend, but that was a really long time ago."

"Are you boyfriend and girlfriend now?"

Stella's face heated. Twelve hours ago, she probably would have been happy to admit they were an item of sorts, but now she wasn't so sure. "No, we're just friends."

"That's too bad. I like Liam from Colorado." Willa spoke over the water as she washed her hands. "He's pretty cool."

"I'm glad you two get along." Stella handed her daughter the hand towel.

As Willa dried her hands and hung the towel back on the hook, she cast a mischievous grin. "Cheyenne's mom got remarried. She said she likes having two dads now. She gets more presents, and she gets to go on two vacations in the summer."

"In all fairness, you get to go on two vacations as well." Stella cocked her head and gave her daughter a look.

"Yeah, I guess that's true." Willa shrugged. "And Aunt Whit says you can't let boys buy your love, they have to earn it."

"Remind me to have a talk with Aunt Whit about her dating advice." Stella shook her head. "Come on, I'm sure Liam's family is waiting."

Walking back through the house, Stella followed the sound of voices drifting in through the screened backdoor. As she stepped out onto the porch, with her daughter in tow, she took in the scene before her. The whole gang was there. She'd seen them all at the wedding, of course, but they'd been mixed among the crowd of guests. Here, however, they were in their element. Relaxed, smiling, laughing with one another.

The men all seemed to be gathered around some sort of project in the yard. A thin, wide piece of wood was stretched out across two shabby sawhorses that looked to be fifty years old and seemed to be serving as a makeshift table. In the grass beside it were stacks of wood in various sizes. She could sense the great man debate all the way up on the porch.

On the patio at the base of the porch steps, the women were gathered around a table, their focus fixed on the baby nestled in Julia's arms. She could only imagine the sense of pride Barbara Scott felt for her first grandchild.

"Stella, it's so good to see you," Barbara crooned as Stella made her way down the steps. "And who is this you have with you?"

"This is my daughter, Willa." Stella wrapped her arm around her daughter and pulled her close, her own pride flaring.

Liam's mother stood and walked over, embracing Stella in a warm hug. Releasing her, she bent slightly and smiled at Willa. "You look just like your mother. Would you like to meet my new granddaughter? Her name is Penelope."

"Sure." Willa took Mrs. Scott's hand and walked with her to the table.

Stella followed and took an empty seat next to Kat. The spring day was warm against her skin. Soon the muggy days of summer would arrive, but for now, the soft breeze made it pleasant to be outside. "That looks pretty intense over there." Stella nodded toward the grass where Liam stood with his father, his three brothers Miles, Drew and Carter, and Kat's husband Brooks.

Kat followed her line of sight and laughed. "Meeting of the minds. In theory, they're building one of those wooden swing sets for Penn. I told dad it was a little too soon, but at this rate, she'll be big enough to use it when they finish. You'd think they'd listen to Drew since he's the carpenter, but he's also the smarta—" Kat hesitated, seeming to realize there were young ears around. "I mean, sarcastic little brother so…"

Stella realized she didn't know much about the family anymore. It had been twelve years since she had really spent time with Liam's younger brothers. The last time she'd seen Drew he was attending the community college, and Carter had just graduated high school. "Drew's a carpenter now?"

"Well, I don't know how much real work he does these days since he owns the company, but yeah, he builds custom homes."

"That's super cool." Willa piped up, glancing over to the group of men. "Can I go see what they're doing?"

"I don't know, sweetie. They seem to be pretty focused."

Kat let out a soft chuckle. "Oh, let her go. She could probably figure it out before they can."

If only Kat knew. Math and problem solving were Willa's hobbies. While most kids were playing video games or riding bikes, Willa was always stuck with her head in a book. Learning was her idea of fun.

Most days, Stella was used to her daughter's gifts, but every now and then, Willa would shock her with some new talent. There was no doubt her daughter would do amazing things in life, but Stella worried about the days ahead. So far, the kids in her school were kind to her, but high school was a grueling place.

Pushing the worries of her daughter's future aside, Stella smiled. "Sure, I guess it's okay."

She watched as her daughter trotted off and inserted herself in the group next to Liam. Instinctively, he wrapped an arm around Willa's shoulders and began pointing at the drawing on the table. Watching the two of them together seemed like the most natural thing in the world.

"He's good with kids." Julia's statement pulled Stella's attention back to the table.

Kat's snicker had all eyes on her. "Maybe with older kids. I let him watch Penn for an hour last night and he had to call in reinforcements."

"He had it handled by the time I got there." Stella tried to reassure Kat, though she was fairly certain the woman wasn't overly worried about her daughter in the hands of her brother. "Willa was pretty colicky when she was a baby."

"It's super fun times." Kat ran a finger down her daughter's arm. "Isn't it, little bird."

"Try having two at one time. I don't think I slept for a year when you and Miles were born," Barbara mused, as she stood from the table. "Come help your mother get dinner out of the oven, Kat. I need Julia to hold that baby and maybe she'll catch the fever. It's about time there's a new generation running around here."

"I told you she was going to be on you next." Kat patted her new sister-in-law on the shoulder as she stood. "Watch out Stella, you'll be next."

Stella's heart sunk to her stomach. Liam could say he didn't want kids all he wanted, but how would he feel when his family and friends started pressuring him. Would it eventually bother him? Would he change his mind?

"We went to Jamaica for a week and it seems like everything changed. So much for this being a sleepy little town." Julia's sweet laughter pulled Stella from her thoughts.

"Yeah, I guess so." Had it really only been a week since Miles and Julia's wedding? Since she'd laid eyes on Liam for the first time in forever? For Stella, it felt like a lifetime.

"So, you two?" Julia raised a brow, and Stella knew exactly what she was asking.

"I don't know." She wasn't sure how to answer the question. Had they been *together*, sure, but that didn't mean they were together as a couple. "It's complicated, I guess."

"Isn't it all." Julia's lips turned into a warm smile. "He brought you home to his parents', so that's gotta say something, right?"

Stella barely knew the woman sitting next to her, but there was something about her kind nature that made Stella feel comfortable. Like she could trust her to the ends of the earth. "It's not a question on his part, I don't think. He seems pretty set on picking up where we left off."

"But you don't know if you can trust him?"

The woman was a mind reader. "Something like that. There's a lot of water under that bridge."

Julia turned her head and glanced out to where her husband stood, before turning her attention back to Stella. "I can respect that. There was a time not too long ago I felt betrayed by Miles. You may not know this, but I was married before. I lost Jason to the war. When I met Miles, I had no idea he had served alongside my husband for years. You know, they don't talk much about what goes on over there. Anyway, Miles figured out who I was, but he never told me. When I found out he'd been there when Jason died, well, it brought up a lot of emotions. The past and the present got all tangled up and it was too much. It took a little soul-searching, and Miles tracking me halfway around the world, but I finally realized life had presented me with a new lease. I just had to accept it."

Stella was fairly certain her jaw was on the floor. "I had no idea."

"Obviously, it all worked out in the end." Julia glanced at her husband across the yard again and smiled. "I guess all I'm saying is sometimes you have to be open to letting the past and the present merge."

Stella wished it were that easy, but the past wasn't fully the problem. She was more concerned about the future. Her trust issues were just the sprinkles on top.

*****

Liam was trying hard not to let Stella's silent treatment get the better of him, but it was a losing battle. Things had seemed perfectly fine through dinner, but she'd hardly spoken a word since they'd pulled out of his parents' driveway. Maybe he was being a total guy, but he didn't have a damn clue what was on her mind. His family had been nothing but welcoming. Sure, they could be overbearing and nosy, but they were nothing if not kind to guests. His mother wouldn't stand for anything less.

How they treated each other, however, was a different story. Sometimes he felt like they were all still kids in school the way they yanked each other's chains. Now that they were both married, Miles and Kat had settled down a bit, but when it came to Drew and Carter, it was a different story. His younger brothers were still living their best lives.

Of course, Liam had been doing the same when he was Carter's age. At thirty-one, his company had been at the height of business. The profits rolling in like the early morning fog. Thick and deep. And he'd had a good time spending those profits, but now he wanted something more substantial than a good time. He wanted what Miles and Kat had. He wanted to settle down. Have someone waiting for him at the end of the day.

It was just too bad that someone wasn't talking to him at the moment. He wanted to ask a million questions, to figure out what was weighing on her mind, but he had a strong feeling it wasn't a conversation to be had in front of Willa.

Thankfully, the kid in the back seat was not above filling the silence. "Papa J says I can come back and help with Penelope's swing set any time I want."

Liam watched out of the corner of his eye as Stella turned in her seat to face her daughter. "Willa, let's not make up nicknames for Liam's family."

"I didn't."

Liam could sense the tension. "It's not her fault. Dad told her to call him Papa J. Apparently, he's trying out grandfather worthy names, but he didn't like our suggestion of Gramps."

"And Drew said I should call Liam, Squeaky." Willa's sweet laughter filled the inside of his truck.

Liam wanted to be pissed at his brother for bringing up his old childhood nickname, but as much as he hated it, he loved the sound of Stella's snicker more. "I forgot they used to call you that."

Liam let out an exaggerated sigh. "If only everyone would forget."

Willa leaned forward from the backseat. "Why did they call you Squeaky anyway?"

"Because they're mean." Liam winked at her in the rearview. "And because my voice went through a squeaky phase when I was in middle school."

"Like a dog toy? Maybe they should have called you Chewy."

"Hey! Whose side are you on here?" Liam protested. "I thought we were friends."

"We are friends, silly." Willa's voice was full of excitement when she spoke again. "I can prove it. Wanna come to Donuts with Dudes at my school on Tuesday? It used to be Donuts with Dads, but some kids don't really have a dad, so now it's just dudes."

Against his will, Liam's heart swelled in his chest. He'd only been messing with her about them being friends, but the thought of her wanting him to show up for some school event made him a little mushy. "That sounds pretty cool, kiddo, but I'm sure your dad will want to be there."

"He can't. He has to go out of town for work." The excitement drained from Willa's voice. "He's always out of town."

Liam's heart sank right along with her voice. The heartbreak in her words twisted in his gut. His parents had rarely missed an event. Even with five kids, they somehow made it work and never missed the important things. He knew Stella was the kind of mom who did her best, but it had to be hard on the kid not having her dad around for the important things.

Before he could agree to come, Stella spoke up from the passenger seat. "I'm sure Liam has a busy schedule."

"But I'll be the only kid without someone there." Willa huffed and sat back against the seat.

From the corner of his eye, he watched Stella reach between the seats and place a gentle hand on her daughter's leg. Had she misunderstood his intention? He would happily go have donuts if it made Willa happy, but something told him he needed to have a conversation with Stella before making any promises.

They drove the last mile to Stella's in silence. He would have promised the kid the world if it would bring back her happy-go-lucky smile, but deep down, he knew it wasn't his place. Pulling into their driveway, Liam put the truck in park and followed the girls up the walkway. As they reach the bottom step, Liam hesitated. He wasn't sure what the protocol was here. He absolutely wanted to pull Stella in his arms and remind her of their evening together, but that didn't exactly fit into the *taking things slow* plan.

Turning to him, Stella's lips turned up into a half smile. "Thanks for taking us to dinner."

"Absolutely, you guys are welcome anytime." Lifting a hand to Willa's head, Liam mused her hair gently. "You think you could give me a minute to talk to your mom?"

A bright smile lit across the girl's face. "Are you going to ask my mom to be your girlfriend now?"

"Willa!" Stella's jaw nearly hit the concrete sidewalk.

Her daughter batted her innocent eyes and shrugged. "It's a valid question."

Wrapping an arm around her daughter's shoulders, Stella ushered Willa up the steps. "Inside, you. I'll be in in a minute to get you ready for bed."

With a huff, Willa unlocked the front door and let herself in. When it was closed tight, Stella turned and headed back down the steps.

"I'm sorry about that." There was no playfulness to her tone.

"She has a point. I haven't asked. Stella James, will you be my girlfriend?"

Chapter Fifteen

Stella had never felt so trapped between a rock and a hard place in her life. There was a twenty-year-old girl inside her that wanted to trust that everything would work out for the best, but she wasn't a young girl anymore.

Life was complicated.

What happened when Liam changed his mind about wanting kids of his own? His mom had been anything but subtle about wanting a houseful of grandkids. What happened when the pressure from his family and his own desire to procreate became too much to deny? Where would that leave them?

Or what if Liam changed his mind about being back in Carefree? He'd spent what felt like a lifetime living in a world full of adventure. What happened when he got bored with the smalltown life? Her life was here. She couldn't just up and leave.

Stella wasn't sure she could handle the heartbreak again, but it was more than just her heart she had to worry about now. Willa was strong in a lot of ways, but her heart was tender. She could see the attachment forming in her daughter's eyes. She was already referring to Liam's father as Papa J. Hell, she'd invited Liam to a school function like he was some sort of stepfather without discussing it with Stella first.

Stella had a responsibility to protect her daughter.

To protect herself.

"Liam, listen...I don't think this thing with Willa is such a good idea." Avoidance wasn't her usual style, but she couldn't answer his question directly. Maybe it was because part of her—a lot of her— wanted to say yes and be whisked off into the sunset.

"You don't think me going to the school is a good idea? Or me hanging out with Willa in general?" His easygoing tone had vanished.

"It's just that I know my daughter. She gets attached really easily. I mean, look at how she was already calling your dad Papa J. It's not fair to let her get attached and then..." Stella let her words drift.

"And then, what?"

She braced herself as Liam took a step closer. The last thing she needed was to get lost in his closeness...again. She had to stick to her guns. Follow her gut. "It will devastate her when this doesn't work out."

Dropping her head, she couldn't bear to look him in the eyes as she spoke the last part aloud. It broke her heart to speak the words, but it was better to rip off the bandage now. Before her life got anymore wrapped up in this fairy tale.

"*When!*" Liam began to pace on the sidewalk. "Stella, what the hell is going on? I thought we were on the same page."

"This doesn't have to be complicated."

"Complicated? The math seems pretty damn simple to me. I want to be with you. You want to be with me. How the hell is that complicated?"

"That's just it. It's not just me and you." Stella felt her temper flare.

"I get that, but last I checked, Willa doesn't seem to have a problem with any of this. She fit right in with my family and they loved her. You know they would treat her as one of their own. Hell, they all but adopted Brooks when we were kids. Family isn't just blood to them."

"You know what I mean." Stella tried to keep her voice calm. Willa was just inside the door and if she knew her daughter, her ear was probably pressed tight to the oak.

"No, I don't know what you mean. I thought we were moving forward. I took you to my parents…is that what this is about? My mom and all her grandkids talk?" Liam scrubbed a hand through his hair. "I told you earlier, I don't care about that."

"You say that now, but Liam, you can't be sure."

"Then we'll cross that bridge when we get there. We can work through whatever life throws at us. Figure out a compromise."

"There is no compromise when it comes to kids. If you change your mind, I can't give you that."

"You're the only one saying I'm going to change my mind here."

Stella watched as he paced along her sidewalk. Her resolve was weakening, but she had to stay strong for her and for Willa. "It's not only that."

"Is this about Willa inviting me to the damn donuts thing?"

The pang of guilt punched Stella in the stomach. She hated the fact that Rick was going to be out of town and wanted nothing more than for Willa to have someone with her at the event, but letting her daughter get closer to Liam wasn't a good idea.

Thanks to the Cheyenne kid in her class sensationalizing the idea of two dads, she could see her daughter's wheels turning. Today had been a mistake. She should have never let her attraction to Liam mix with her personal life. It was another reason she needed to break this off now. She didn't make wise choices when it came to him. And Willa was putting a lot of stock in Liam without knowing he had a propensity to leave when the going got tough.

"About that…" Stella thought through her words carefully. She couldn't be sure how much her daughter was hearing on the other side of the door. Lowering her voice, Stella continued, "I think it's for the best if you tell her you're busy. The last thing she needs is to get attached and then you disappear."

Liam stopped pacing and looked her dead in the eye. She could see the tension bunching in his shoulders. His frustration rolled off him in waves.

When he spoke, his voice was harsh. "Be honest. This has nothing to do with Willa and everything to do with your own insecurities."

His words felt like a slap across the face. Anger burned deep in her gut. "You mean the insecurities gifted to me by you men. You left. My father left. Rick's only around half the time. It's all you men do. You make promises and then leave. Excuse me for trying to protect my daughter from that. From a lifetime of pain and disappointment."

*****

"Stella..." Liam's shoulders dropped as the edge in his voice vanished.

Until that moment, he hadn't realized how much the past still haunted her. How deep the abandonment ran. Fear and pain swirled in her wild eyes. Like a dredger pulling sand from the dark depths of the ocean, he'd brought all the hurt back to the surface.

All he wanted was to make her believe he was here, and yet his words strummed the chords of regret. Foolishly, he'd jumped in head first and expected her to follow. And when she hadn't, his emotions had gotten the best of him.

All the back and forth was killing him.

Every time he thought they were making progress, taking a step forward, she was taking two steps back. The harder he pushed, the faster she retreated.

How many times could they do this? Fall in each other's arms only to have her pull away. He wanted so much to fix what he had broken, but it would take more than his desire to repair the damage.

He loved her, and God help him, he loved that kid, but she would never forgive him.

With defeat beating on his door, Liam steadied his voice. "I wish I could take back all the pain I caused, I really do. I wish I could change the way things went down...but no amount of wishing can change the past. I love you, I always have...but I don't know if it's enough."

Her words were as quiet as the night. "I don't know either. I just need some time to think."

"Right." Liam scrubbed a hand through his hair. What else could he say to that? No matter how much he wanted this, he couldn't make her want it too. When he spoke again, his words were far calmer than the storm raging inside him. "Well, it's a school night, so you should probably get Willa in bed."

"I should."

He was leaving a piece of his heart on her sidewalk, and there wasn't shit he could do about it. Not at the moment. If she wanted time, time was what he would give her.

The following afternoon, Liam drove the passenger van down the drive and parked next to the Pebble Creek mansion. He'd never felt so exhausted after an excursion in his life. The Stanley Group had been amazing, with only one member of the party getting sick on the open water, but his heart hadn't been in it.

He'd slept like shit and been up before the sun. All he wanted was to go home and crash on his couch for the next three days.

Stepping from the van, he took in the sight of the tiny figure sitting on the dock by the boathouse. He couldn't be sure from the distance, but he was guessing from her posture she wasn't happy. Pushing the thought aside for the moment, Liam helped the group unload their gear from the back of the van.

As he stepped around to the passenger side, he was greeted with Whitney's presence. "How'd it go?"

"Pretty good. Only had one feeding the fish with their breakfast."

"There's always one." Whitney chuckled and then her face turned serious. "So, what the hell happened?"

Liam glanced over her shoulder to the group retreating into the mansion. Confused, he glanced back to her. "What do you mean? Everything went well. Did someone complain?"

He couldn't imagine that anyone had contacted her to complain about the trip. They had all seemed pleased, and he hadn't heard anyone making any calls. How would word have gotten back to Whitney without him knowing?

"I'm not talking about the fishing trip. What happened yesterday? When Stella picked Willa up, she said you were joining them for lunch. She seemed nervous, but excited about it. Now they're not speaking and you look like hell."

"What do you mean they're not speaking?" It was one thing for him and Stella to have a tiff, but what did it have to do with Willa?

"Stella's been in a mood all day and asked if I could get Willa from school. When I picked her up, I asked Willa what was going on because she seemed off. She muttered something about donuts, and her mom being mean." Whitney shrugged. "I didn't really think much about it, but then when we got back here, she went down to the dock and has been down there for half an hour. She always goes straight to Stella's office so I tried to ask Stella what was going on, and she blew me off. Now I'm asking you what the hell happened?"

Liam let out a heavy sigh. He knew exactly what was going on. Stella had told Willa he couldn't go with her to the Dudes and Donuts event. The only problem was Willa fighting with her mom over this was not going to help his cause. Stella was already concerned about Willa getting too attached. Willa picking his side, so to speak, was not going to make matters any better.

He had to smooth things over before Willa completely tanked his already sinking ship. "Where's Stella now?"

"In her office on a call, but I gotta warn you, she's in a serious mood."

He couldn't worry about that at the moment. Stella had wanted time to think, and he would give her that. Willa on the other hand, he could reason with. "Understood, she's not the James woman I need to talk to right now."

Whitney cocked her head and shot him a curious look. "Tread lightly," she warned.

"Got it."

Heading out across the yard, Liam jogged his way to the dock. As he approached, he slowed to a walk, collecting his thoughts.

"Well, if it isn't my favorite nine-year-old," Liam called as he stepped on to the dock.

Willa turned toward him, and a weak smile spread across her lips. "I'm the only nine-year-old you know."

"True. Guess that makes you my favorite and least favorite all in one."

"You're ridiculous." Willa turned her focus back to the water.

"So I've been told." Liam took a seat next to her and let his legs dangle over the dock. Staring out over the water, he asked the question he already knew the answer to. "Wanna tell me what's going on?"

"Mom said you couldn't come to the breakfast. I'm going to be the only kid there that doesn't have somebody to sit with them, and it's not fair."

The crack in her voice ripped through his heart. This kid was going to be the death of him, but he couldn't take the pain in her voice.

"Can you keep a secret? A real secret." From his peripheral, he saw her body perk up.

"I'm the best secret keeper."

Stella was going to kill him if she ever found out, but it was a risk he had to take. There was no way he was going to let Willa sit there all alone with no one by her side. This kid deserved the world. Stella may not be ready to accept he was there for her, but he could be there for Willa.

There was a strong chance this would blow up in his face if Stella found out, but for now it would be their little secret. He knew on a deep level asking Willa to lie to her mom was wrong, but it wasn't like they were committing a crime. He was going to eat a donut and tell terrible jokes with her friends. What was the harm in that?

"The truth is, I broke your mom's heart a long time ago. I made some pretty dumb decisions and now she has a hard time trusting I won't do it again. She's not wrong to have doubts."

Willa turned to him, curiosity coloring her face. "What dumb decisions?"

A soft laugh rattled from his chest. "That's a story for another day, when you're old and gray. Here's the thing, you have to promise not to tell your mom I'm coming. She won't be happy if she finds out, and lying is terrible, so this is the one and only time we're going to forget to mention it. Okay?"

In a blink, Willa's arms flung around his neck and squeezed tight. Hugging her back, Liam couldn't help but feel like he'd sealed his own fate, but the joy radiating from Willa was worth it. Now, he had to pray like hell Stella never found out.

"Is that a promise?" Liam asked when she pulled back.

Making a zipper motion across her lips, Willa twisted her fingers like a key engaging a lock and threw it out over the water. "Your secret's safe with me."

Chapter Sixteen

Stella tried her damnedest to concentrate on the voice coming through the phone, but the scene through her office window was sucking all of her attention. Willa hadn't bothered to come to Stella's office when she'd returned from school which broke her heart, but now her daughter was sitting on the dock with the one person Stella couldn't face today.

She wanted to go out there and find out what they were up to, but that meant coming face to face with Liam and she wasn't ready for that. After their fight the previous night, she wasn't sure where they stood. She wasn't even sure where she wanted them to stand. Her heart wanted to trust that Liam had changed, that he was really here to stay, but she couldn't escape the nagging feeling it was a ticking time bomb.

Her emotions were giving her whiplash.

Pushing the drama that was her love life aside, Stella forced the cheerfulness in her voice. "Absolutely, I would be happy to come serve donuts at the event. What time should I be there?"

Susan, the PTO president, chirped happily. "We're going to get setup right after the bell rings. If you want to join us in the cafeteria after you drop Willa off, that would be perfect,"

"I'll see you then." It wasn't her proudest moment, but the fight with Willa about Liam not coming was weighing on Stella. Being there to watch over Willa gave her a small sense that her daughter wouldn't be alone.

Just as Stella hit end on her phone and took a seat at her desk, the door to her office opened and Whitney appeared. "The Stanley group is back. Seems the fishing trip was a success for everyone, minus their finance guru. I don't think she'll be going out for round two anytime soon."

Stella fought the urge to walk back over to the window to see if Liam was still out there. "Great."

"That's all?" Whitney took a seat across from Stella's desk. "You aren't interested to know anything else?"

Stella wasn't in the mood for trick questions or games. "Should I be?"

"Well, I thought maybe you'd want to know whether a certain ex looked like sunshine and rainbows or shit reheated in the microwave, but I guess I was wrong."

"As long as our guests had a good time, that's all I'm interested in." Stella studied the monitor on her desk and tried to ignore the truth. Of course she wanted to know everything about Liam, especially what he was doing on the dock with Willa, but she couldn't go down that road. She needed to get her act together. She was too old for this emotional rollercoaster. "We have two weeks before our next excursion. I think that should give us time to find someone else to fill in until Jackson is back on his feet."

Whitney's face twisted in confusion. "Okay, out with it. What happened yesterday? And don't tell me nothing. You showed up at my house with the morning after glow and left excited to have lunch with Liam, so what happened? Is it something with Willa, because I will walk out there and kick his ass right now."

"No." The word came out with more force than she intended. "He's great with her. It's nothing like that."

"Then what is it? Because something's not adding up."

Stella stood and glanced out the window in time to see Willa's arms wrap around Liam's neck, and her heart skipped a beat. She wanted to be furious. She wanted to stomp out there and demand to know what was going on, but all she could feel was the kindness he'd shown her daughter.

She'd known the moment Willa had walked out to the dock instead of coming to her office that her daughter was still mad. Stella had planned to go out and smooth things over, but before she could the phone had rung. Now, it was Liam comforting her daughter, making Willa feel better.

And wasn't that just the problem?

Liam was a good guy.

Yes, they had a past that was less than desirable, but the man who'd shown up out of the blue was kind, caring, and…honest.

Dammit! She was supposed to be getting off the rollercoaster, not taking it for another spin.

"I'll tell you what the problem is." Stella paced. "The man shows up after twelve years of silence. Twelve years, Whit, twelve. And thinks we can pick up where we left off like none of it ever happened. It's been a few weeks, and somehow, he magically knows I'm the only one for him. That's insane."

Whitney smiled and shrugged her shoulders. "I don't know, I think it's kind of romantic."

"Yeah, well, this is not the *Hallmark Channel.* My life is not some rom-com movie. We can't parade around the town square for three days and then live happily ever after. I have a business, and a daughter…and a shit-ton of trust issues."

Whitney's laughter filled the office. "When you say it like that, it kind of sounds like the plot to a movie."

Stella plopped down in her chair. "I'm serious."

"I know." Whitney leaned forward and reached her hands across the desk in a show of support. "But what's the harm in seeing where it goes?"

"The harm is…I don't know if I can survive another heartbreak."

"And what if it's not another heartbreak? What if this is the exact moment you're supposed to get the happily ever after you've always wanted, and you're not even willing to take the chance?"

A massive headache was brewing at the base of Stella's skull. "You don't know that."

"You're right, I don't, but I do know the way that man looks at you when you're not watching. And I also know he's out there trying to cheer up Willa because he cares almost as much about her as he cares about you. And just in case I need to spell it out for ya, it means he cares a helluva lot for you, because if he wasn't planning on sticking around, he wouldn't give two shits about your daughter or her feelings."

Shit, she hated when Whitney had a logical point. "But it's not only my feelings I have to be concerned with. I have to think about Willa in all of this too."

"And you'd be a terrible mother if you didn't, but if you think she's going to go through life without getting her feelings hurt or ever being disappointed, think again. Look, I'm not a mom, so maybe I don't have a leg to stand on here, but isn't part of raising a daughter teaching her how to deal with the shit life throws at you? She doesn't need you to be perfect. She needs you to show her how to get back up when life knocks you down. She needs you to teach her how to accept whatever life has to offer. And most of all, she needs to see you fail and survive, so she knows failure is okay."

Stella chuckled. "Well, I think I have the failure thing down pat, so we can check that one off the list."

"You don't give yourself enough credit, James. You've done amazing things, against some pretty impressive odds. Of course, you couldn't have done it without me, but this isn't about me." Whitney tilted her head and shrugged. "Now, what do you say I pick up takeout and bring it over tonight. After Willa goes to bed, we can watch one of those sappy rom-coms and figure out what you're going to do next."

Before Stella could reject Whitney's proposal, Willa's face appeared in the office doorway. The quiet squeak of the hinge had Whitney's head turning on a swivel. "Hey kiddo, I'm bringing over takeout. What do you think, Chinese or Italian?"

So much for turning Whitney down. If Stella said no, it would be the second time in as much as a day she'd played the bad guy in her daughter's eyes.

A sweet smile spread across Willa's lips. "Make it Japanese and you have yourself a deal."

"You drive a hard bargain." Whitney stood from her chair. "I'm guessing you want spring rolls, too?"

Willa beamed. "They're the best part."

Whitney shook her head, but smiled. "Well, I guess I should be thankful you don't have the typical nine-year-old palate of chicken nuggets and cheeseburgers."

Stella waited for Whitney to exit her office before opening her mouth. "Hey sweet girl, how was your day?"

Willa took a seat on the couch and shrugged. "It was fine."

Stella was well aware her daughter was not happy about the whole Liam situation, but a small part of her had hoped Willa would be over it by now. "Did something else happen or are you still upset about our conversation this morning?"

On the way to school, Stella had tried to delicately explain why it was inappropriate to invite

Liam to a school function, but that had proved to be a harder conversation than she thought. Of course, it didn't help that the only reason she didn't want him to show up was based purely on her own insecurities.

"School was fine. Just school." Willa shrugged again.

So, this was all about Liam. "Wil, about tomorrow—"

"It's okay, Mom. My friend Ella said I could sit with her and her dad. Did you know he works for a candy company? He always brings candy when he comes to have lunch with her. Maybe he'll bring some tomorrow to go with our donuts."

"I didn't know that." Stella cringed at the idea of donuts and candy all before nine a.m. That poor teacher was going to have to make the kids run laps around the playground to burn off the excess energy from so many sweets.

On a brighter note, Stella was happy to see Willa was coming around, but she had a feeling it had more to do with whatever was said on the dock and less to do with her friend's dad bringing candy.

Which brought her to the next topic of conversation.

Stella wanted to know what had happened to make Willa hug Liam so, but she wasn't ready to confess she'd seen their little moment.

Stella tried to keep her voice indifferent. "What were you doing outside?"

"Just hanging out on the dock."

Any other day, Willa would have been spilling her guts, but of course, since Stella wanted to know what they had been discussing, her daughter wasn't talking. "I saw Liam was down there with you."

At the mention of Liam's name, Willa lifted her chin. "Yeah, I think he was bringing the people back, but he's gone now."

Well, at least Stella had the answer to one of her questions. She wouldn't have to spend the night hiding in her office, trying to avoid him. "So, what were you guys talking about?"

"Nothing really, he came to say hi."

As for why Liam had gone down to the dock, it looked like Stella wasn't getting that answer unless she went straight to the source.

And she was not about to do that.

*****

Liam took a seat at the bar next to his younger brother, Drew. "No hot date?"

"I reserve my dating life to the weekends. I'm too tired during the week for anything more than a cold beer and *ESPN*." Drew picked up the long neck bottle in front of him and took a draw. "Speaking of dating, I'm surprised you answered when I called. I figured you'd be with Stella."

Liam ordered a stiff drink from the bartender before turning back to his brother. "To be honest, I was heading for my couch, so you're lucky you called when you did."

"Trouble in paradise already?" Drew nudged him with his elbow.

"Something like that."

"Damn brother, you two seemed good yesterday at Mom and Dad's. Must have been a rough night. You know, there's plenty of studying material on the internet if you need some pointers."

"Trust me, there's no complaints in that department." Sex with Stella was definitely not the issue. It was the only time they seemed to be on the same page.

Drew dropped his playful tone. "So, what happened?"

"Specifically? Willa asked me to come to this event at her school tomorrow. It's some dudes and donuts thing where the kids have donuts with a male figure in their life, I guess."

"Okay…so what's the problem? Did you tell the kid no?"

"That's the thing, I'm happy to go, but Stella is worried about Willa getting too attached. Said it would be hard on her if things went south. Needless to say, it brought up a lot of shit from the past, and let's just say it didn't end well."

"So, what are you going to do?" Liam was quiet for a long moment. Long enough for Drew to sense something was up. "Oh shit, what did you do?"

Liam let out a heavy sigh. His brother wasn't going to tattle on him, so what was the harm in telling Drew the truth? "Stella asked me not to go. And I was fine with it. But then I got back to the mansion today and Willa was down on the dock. I could tell something was up, so I went to check on her. She was upset that she's the only kid who won't have anyone there tomorrow because her dad is out of town."

"Tell me you didn't?"

"You didn't see the disappointment in her eyes. When's the last time you had to tell a nine-year-old girl to suck it up because life blows sometimes? That shit ain't easy. Wrestling a crocodile would be easier."

"I'll take your word for it." Drew let out a small laugh. "So, now Stella's pissed, which is why you're here with me and not hanging out with her."

Liam stared at the flat screen hanging above the bar without seeing what was on the TV. He was up shit creek without a paddle and knew it. "She's not pissed...yet."

"You didn't tell her?" Drew's voice cut through the noise of the crowded restaurant.

"Could you yell that shit a little louder?" Liam glanced around to see if anyone was listening.

His conscience was getting the better of him. No one here would know Stella, much less what they were talking about. She lived in Pebble Creek, not Carefree, and if he had to guess, Stella's friend list probably didn't include middle aged men hanging out in a sports bar on a Monday afternoon.

Picking up his whiskey, Liam took a long drink, finishing the contents of the glass. "The words were out of my mouth before I knew what I was saying, and then Willa hugged me. I couldn't take it back. That would've been ten times worse than me not going in the first place. If I tell Stella what I did, she'll make me undo it or worse she'll undo it herself, and I don't want to cause trouble between them."

"You know she's going to have your balls on a platter when she finds out. You can't go messing around with someone's kid like that. Even I know that much."

The knot in Liam's gut twisted tighter. "I know, but what the hell am I supposed to do now?"

"For starters, you should probably go say your goodbyes to Mom and Dad tonight."

"Not helpful." Liam lifted his hand and waved for the bartender to bring them another round.

"What if you ask Dad to go instead? They seemed to hit it off last night. It would get you off the hook and the kid wouldn't have to sit by herself."

Liam wished he would have thought of that before he stuck his foot in his mouth. Stella didn't want him there, but maybe she would have been more receptive to his dad showing up for Willa. Although, Stella wasn't too keen on Willa calling him Papa J, so it probably wouldn't have worked either.

There was also the small problem that at the end of the day, Liam wanted to go. He never would have guessed being invited to a school function would have had such an effect on him, but the truth was, he was excited Willa had asked him.

"I'm not dragging Dad into my mess."

"Well, then I guess we only have two options. Start writing your apology speech or plan your funeral."

His brother wasn't wrong about the funeral, but after their last conversation, Liam wasn't sure Stella would ever really forgive him, whether he showed up at the school or not. She had a Texas size chip on her shoulder and no matter how many steps he thought they were taking, she was always ready to run in the other direction.

"Just don't let them bury me in some cheap suit."

Chapter Seventeen

Thank goodness Stella had made the drive to Pebble Creek Elementary a million times, because her mind was anything but focused. Largely in part to the bottle of pinot she'd devoured the night before. When would she learn trying to keep up with Whitney's ability to consume fermented grapes was a terrible idea?

Even with her sunglasses, Stella squinted against the bright morning sun as she pulled into the student drop off zone. Glancing over her shoulder, she pasted what she hoped was a convincing smile across her lips. "Have a wonderful day."

"Thanks, Mom!" Willa chirped before opening the door and hopping out.

Maybe it was the hangover clouding her head, but Willa seemed to be taking this whole thing in stride. It was too bad Stella hadn't known her daughter would get over it so easily before she'd agreed to help out this morning. The last thing she needed was to be serving donuts to half the town, in a loud cafeteria, when she could still feel the wine swirling in her system.

Pulling out of the drop off line, Stella circled around to the visitor lot and parked her car. With a few minutes to spare, she closed her eyes and stilled herself in the silence, willing the ibuprofen to kick in.

True to form, her moment of tranquility didn't last. In the seat next to her, Stella's phone vibrated against the leather. Grabbing it, she stared at the photo Willa had taken of Whitney last summer out on the boat and set as Whit's contact image. Even in a still photo, her best friend radiated eternal optimism. As though nothing life threw at her could ever break her stride. Stella wished she had half as much faith that life would work itself out.

With a deep breath, she answered the phone. "I'm not chickening out. I'm going to talk to him today."

Whitney's laugh trickled through the phone. "For the record, that's not why I'm calling. But since you brought it up, don't forget the part where you told me you are still madly in love with him."

"I admitted I had feelings for him. I never said I was madly in love."

"Same difference." Whitney changed the subject before Stella could rebut. "Anyway, I'm calling because I just received a very interesting phone call and I think you're going to want to call them back."

It was too early to argue about semantics or her feelings for Liam. "Whit, I told you I'm volunteering this morning. Whatever it is will have to wait until I get back to the office."

"Okay, I guess I'll tell the creative director of Sweet Home Sawyer you're too busy to take her call."

Stella's heart skipped a beat. *Sweet Home Sawyer* was one of her favorite home design TV shows, but why were they calling her? Sawyer Linden remodeled old homes in the Atlanta suburbs. Not plantations turned event centers in the middle of nowhere South Carolina. Not that Pebble Creek needed work anyway.

"You couldn't have led with that?" Stella barked through the phone.

"Ehh, probably, but then I wouldn't have had a chance to poke the bear." A soft laugh filled the line. "Anyway, I emailed you her contact info. She said she would be in meetings most of the day, so you might not want to wait."

"I'll give her a call now before I head in." Stella's mind was whirling. "And Whit."

"Yeah?"

"Thanks."

"Of course, it's not every day a TV show calls."

"I meant more for listening to me whine about my love life." As reluctant as she'd been to admit the truth, there was a new sense of calm having said the words aloud. The part of her that had held on to the memory of Liam would always love the boy she'd met in college, but it was more than that. She loved the man he'd become. He was open and honest. The kind of man that loved deeply. And as hard as it was to let go of her insecurities, she knew she could trust him at his word.

"Well, I mean, it was listen to you blather on or accept a date invite from the supposed plastic surgeon who can't seem to spell simple English words correctly, but wants to be my sugar daddy. It was a tough choice, really."

"I don't even want to know what that means." Stella shook her head. This was precisely why she would never join a dating app. "Okay, let me call the show back before I'm super late and end up on the PTO naughty list. We'll talk when I get back to the office."

With that, Stella hung up the call and opened her email. As promised, Whitney had sent over all the contact information for the creative director of Sweet Home Sawyer, Stacy Weldon. Her mind sifted through every possible scenario of what they could want with her, but there was only one way to find out. Tapping the number highlighted in blue, Stella placed the call on speaker phone.

A moment later, a young woman who sounded like she couldn't have been a day out of college answered the call, announcing the name of the production company. Stella relayed she was returning a call and was transferred.

"Stacy Weldon." The woman's voice had an air of annoyance.

"Hi, Miss Weldon. My name is Stella James, from Pebble Creek Plantation. My assistant said you were trying to reach me."

"Of course, Stella, hi." The annoyed tenor was replaced with a pleasant tone. "I really appreciate you getting back to me so quickly. Listen, I'm on a tight schedule so I'm going to get right to it. As you may know, I'm the creative director for Sweet Home Sawyer. Are you familiar with the show?"

Familiar? She'd seen every episode. Stella still couldn't believe she was talking to someone who worked directly with Sawyer. "Of course, who isn't?"

"Great! That'll save me some time explaining things. We're looking to do something a little different for our Christmas special this year. A bit of rebranding, if you will, in light of Sawyer's split with her ex. I'm going to assume you've read the tabloids or any news website in the past two weeks."

Although Sawyer was the star of the show, the fact that she was married to the famed pitcher of the *Atlanta Braves* had always been a big part of the show. Stella wasn't into sports, so that had never mattered to her. She didn't care about the celebrity part. For her, it was all about Sawyer's designs. They were sleek and modern, and still somehow cozy and inviting. Whitney, however, was all about the celebrity gossip and could no doubt fill her in later.

"Long story short, the special will be a two-part series covering the renovation of a bed and breakfast. We had hundreds of businesses submit, and the one we've chosen is the Saxton House located in Carefree. Have you heard of the place?"

Her mind swirled. "I'm familiar with the bed and breakfast, but I'm afraid I don't understand what that has to do with me or Pebble Creek?"

"We need a place to set up shop, a home base of sorts while we're filming, and my location scout brought your place to my attention. On paper, it checks a lot of boxes. A place for some of the crew to stay, meeting spaces perfect for planning, plus the backdrop would be great for some of the commentary shots. Filming would take roughly six weeks and we would compensate well."

Six weeks? There was no way Stella had six weeks of open schedule any time this year. She only booked weddings two weekends out of the month, and most of those were in the summer months, but she already had other events and contracts booked throughout the year.

"Before you say anything." Stacy continued, interrupting Stella's mild panic attack. "I'd like to come out and see the place with my own eyes. I'm sure your business is lovely, but photos online can be a bit deceiving. It will also give us a chance to discuss things in more detail. I'm sure you will think of a hundred questions the moment we hang up. Myself and some of the team are going to be in the area at the end of next week for planning and prep. The non-glamorous part of the process. Would you be available anytime Thursday or Friday?"

"Wow, this is a lot to take in." Stella wished there was someone in the car to pinch her because no way this was really happening. A national show wanted to use Pebble Creek for staging and filming. She had to be dreaming. "I can make myself available whenever it's best for you."

Outside her car window, Stella watched as men of various ages parked and headed toward the school for the breakfast. She despised being late, always priding herself on her punctuality, but this was huge. Sawyer Linden might be staying on her estate. Better yet, part of *Sweet Home Sawyer* might be shot on her property. The potential impact this could have was massive.   Madam Susan and her band of overachieving PTO moms would just have to wait.

"I'd like to see the place in full light. How about we plan for one o'clock on Friday?"

Stella accessed the calendar app on her phone. "Friday is perfect." Although there was always work to be done, she didn't have any meetings scheduled. "Is there anything I can do or have ready to better help you?"

"That won't be necessary. You're doing more than enough by accommodating us on such short notice. The only thing I would suggest, however, is write down any questions you have between now and then. It can be a little overwhelming and you might forget some of the things you wanted to ask."

"Excellent idea." There were already a million questions racing through her mind.

"I hate to cut this short, but I have another meeting to get to. We'll see you Friday."

Dropping her phone in her purse, a massive smile spread across Stella's face. Whitney and Willa were going to lose their minds when they found out. Hell, Stella was kind of losing her own mind right now. A celebrity might be staying at Pebble Creek. For six weeks.

Oh God! What if Sawyer was part of the team that was coming next week? She'd never geeked out about celebrities, but now that she might meet one, she kind of was. There was so much to do, so much to think about, but first, she had to get through this breakfast.

At least the rush from the phone call had cured her hangover. It was hard to feel half dead when you were floating in the clouds.

Nothing could ruin this day.

*****

With his name scribbled on the visitor's log, Liam placed the volunteer sticker he'd been handed onto his shirt, and entered the seventh circle of hell. The cafeteria was reminiscent of his own elementary school. The cinderblock walls coated in decades of off-white paint so thick you could barely see the textured pattern. The stainless-steel serving line ran the length of the right-hand wall, while the left side was constructed of tall windows, and in between was a vibrating sea of kids excited to be doing anything other than school work.

"Which classroom are you looking for?" Liam turned to find a shorter woman with sandy blonde hair smiling up at him. She couldn't have been more than five-two, and nearly blended in with the kids. "If you tell me the class, I can point you in the right direction."

Shit, Willa hadn't told him who her teacher was. "I'm not sure, actually. I'm here for Willa James." This earned him a curious look. Had Stella warned them not to let him in?

"Of course." The woman was sizing him up. "Are you..." her words lingered with an unspoken question.

Thankfully, he'd had his coffee this morning, because it only took a second for Liam to catch on where this conversation was headed. "A friend of the family. Willa's dad is out of town on business, so I'm filling in."

"Right, that's very sweet of you...I'm sorry, I didn't catch your name?"

Because he hadn't given it to her. "Liam."

"Well, Liam, Mrs. Moore's class is over in the left corner."

Liam followed the direction her dainty hand pointed and locked on to the sight of Willa waving from her table. A bright smile lit her little face like a kid on Christmas.

"Thanks, I got it from here."

Making his way through the chaos, Liam was greeted with a tight hug the moment he reached the table. "You made it." Willa's smile grew wider.

"I'm not going to lie, I tried to bail at the door, but that woman wouldn't let me back out." Liam glanced around the room. "This is a lot of kids."

"It's just the third graders." Willa spoke the words as though there were only a handful of kids in the room.

"What? No donuts for the other kids?" Not that he wanted to be in here with the entire school. One grade was loud enough.

"They do one grade a month. It should have been our turn last month, but they let fifth grade go before us, which isn't fair," Willa whined.

Liam smiled inwardly at the world problems of a nine-year-old. If only his worries were as simple as someone getting to have a donut before him. "I'm sure there was a reason."

"Probably." Willa shrugged. "But I guess it's kind of good. I didn't know you last month and if my dad was out of town, I wouldn't have had anyone to invite. Well, maybe Jackson, but he's kind of like a big kid, not really an adult."

"So, how does this work? Do we go up and get donuts or do people bring them to us?" Liam glanced around the room to see if there was any sense of order to things. It appeared as though most of the tables were now full with kids and adults.

"They'll come around and tell us when it's our turn to go."

"And what do we do while we wait?" It occurred to him that he hadn't actually inquired any information other than when to show up. He had no idea what the point was of the event.

"I don't know, just hangout." Willa shifted in her seat.

On the opposite end of their table, an elderly man sat with what Liam assumed was his grandson. The kid was showing off some sort of playing cards with cartoon characters on them. Maybe he should have brought something with him. Perhaps a deck of cards. Not that poker was probably allowed in school.

Thrumming his fingers against the table, Liam tried to think of something they could do. "What do you say to a game of I Spy while we wait our turn?"

"I say I get to go first." Willa's eyes lit and began searching the room.

"Hey!" Liam protested jokingly. "How come you get to go first?"

"Because I'm the kid." Willa's smile was more than a little mischievous. "Ready?"

"Fine, but take it easy on me. I'm an old man." Liam grimaced when the actual old man at the table shot him a disapproving look.

It took five guesses and two hints, but five minutes later he finally guessed the correct blue shirt in the room. "Okay, my turn. I spy..."

Liam turned in his seat and began to examine the room when his eyes fell upon his demise. The short blonde was making a beeline toward Stella, who'd just entered the door. A smile was plastered on the tiny woman's face. He'd seen this movie before. The woman wanted to know who he was, and she was going straight for the source. Like a silent film, he watched the scene playout. The woman's hand reaching out and landing softly on Stella's arm as a show of trust and friendship. The sweet, innocent smile luring her in with a false sense of security. And then her lips parted. The words that would bring him to his end flowing from her tongue. Right on cue, Stella's eyes lifted. "Oh shit."

"Ummm, potty words aren't allowed at school."

At the sound of Willa's words, Liam turned back to her, his mind racing. "Right, my bad."

But it was too late, she was already looking over his shoulder to see what he was talking about. "Oh crap!"

Chapter Eighteen

Stella pushed back the bile rising in her throat as she stared across the cafeteria. She had explicitly told Liam not to come, and yet, there he sat with Willa across the table from him. Both their gazes locked on her.

That's right buddy, you're a dead man.

If there weren't a room full of witnesses, she'd drag him out by his collar and kick his ass all the way back to Carefree, but unfortunately, that wasn't an option. At least, not at the moment.

"So…"

Stella turned to find Susan, president of the PTA and gossip club, staring at her in wait. "I'm sorry, what were you saying?"

"Oh, don't play coy." Susan waved her tiny little nimble finger and laughed. "Who's the hunk?"

"Yes, do tell." Sherri with an *i* and two divorced husbands joined the conversation.

This was the last thing Stella needed. Susan and her gang of nosy moms were all staring at her, waiting for an answer. "Liam's an old friend from college."

"Is that what the cool kids are calling it these days? An old friend?" Susan wagged her brows.

Whatever she and Liam may have been was none of their business, because whatever it was, it was no more. She'd asked for one thing, and he couldn't even give her that.

"If having an old friend fill in for Willa's father, who's out of town, is what people are calling it, then I guess so, Susan." Her anger at Liam was momentarily redirected toward the prying women.

"Well." Sherri's lips twisted into a devilish smile. "I'll ask if no one else is going to. Is he single? I could use a little one-on-one time with a man like that."

A twist of emotion tangled in Stella's gut. As far as she was concerned, Liam was as single as the day he'd entered the world, but she wasn't about to feed that information to the woman who was always on the hunt for her next ex-husband. Stella was angry, not a savage who was about to feed him to the lion…or cougar as it were.

Or maybe she should.

It would serve him right to have to fend off the not-so-subtle passes Sherri would undoubtedly give him. The woman was like a heat seeking missile whenever there was a single, hot-blooded man in the room. Once her target was locked, there was no escape.

"Well, as luck would have it, he does happen to be single. He just sold his company, and moved back to Carefree." Stella could see the dollar signs flash in Sherri's eyes. A wealthy bachelor was better than a broke one.

"Maybe I should go introduce myself. Southern hospitality and all. If it's a sweet treat he's after, I have just the thing." Sherri straightened her shoulders and perked up her chest as a smile spread across her cherry red lips.

"I hope your friend has a good head on his shoulders." Susan sighed as they watched Sherri saunter across the cafeteria.

The fact that he was here, against her wishes, was not a good indication he had half a brain between his ears. With nothing else to be done on the matter at the moment, Stella turned her attention back to Susan. "Should we start serving the donuts?"

"Of course, I think most of the men have arrived."

For fifteen minutes, Stella put on her best professional face and served donuts as the students and their guests came through the line one table at a time. The amount of energy it took to ignore Cherry Lip Sherri circling Liam's table was exhausting Stella's already tired body.

She barely had enough energy to be furious as it was. If only she could go back a few weeks to the night of Miles and Julia's wedding. There were so many things she would have done differently. For starters, she would have left and let Whitney handle all the cleanup. Then she wouldn't be in this mess in the first place.

As Willa's table approached the line, Stella's heart pounded against her chest. She needed to keep her cool.

"Hey Mom." Willa's voice was quiet and full of guilt.

Guilt that broke Stella's heart. This wasn't her fault. "Hey sweet girl, are you having fun?" Stella did her best to be uplifting and cheerful as she placed her daughter's favorite donut on her plate.

"Uh, I guess so." Willa's face twisted in confusion.

"Stella, I—" Liam began, but she wasn't having this conversation here, not with Susan's ears prying.

"Not now." Her words were barely a whisper, but stern.

"But Mom—"

Before Willa could get the words out of her mouth, Stella handed the tongs to Susan. "Can you take over for a second?"

Stella didn't wait for an answer. She needed to head this off, and quickly. Walking around the far end of the table, she bent down and stared her daughter in the eyes. "Listen, what's done is done. Now, go enjoy yourself and that yummy donut." She tapped a light finger on the end of Willa's nose and smiled.

"You're not mad at me?"

She could see the tears threatening to escape. "No baby, I'm not mad at you. But I will be sad if you don't get to enjoy this time, so head back over to your table and I will see you at pick up this afternoon, okay? I love you. To the moon and back." With that,

Stella pressed a quick kiss on her daughter's cheek and rose.

"I love you too, Mom."

She waited for Willa to take a few steps away before locking eyes with Liam. "Since lying seems to be your forte, you better go convince her everything is fine, or she'll spend the entire day worrying she's in trouble. And for the record, that's on you."

"Stel—"

"Just go. You have some convincing to do."

*****

Liam knew there was a chance Stella would find out about this whole charade, but never in a million years had he expected her to be at the school. Shit, he should have thought this through. Drew was right, he should have written a damn apology speech. Not that she would even let him get a word in. He needed to talk to her, but Stella was right, this wasn't the place.

Walking back to the table, Liam put his game face on. The last thing he wanted was Willa worrying about this all day. The problems between him and Stella weren't something the kid needed to worry about.

"These look amazing, huh?" Liam sat his plate on the table and took a seat.

"She's mad, isn't she?"

This wasn't going to be an easy sell. "No, it's all good."

"You're lying." Willa poked at the donut in front of her.

Liam could feel Stella's eyes boring in the back of his skull. At least, he was ninety-nine percent sure they were. He was already up shit creek for not doing what she said once, and he didn't need to pile on to the list by not convincing Willa, but the kid was observant. "You're a smart kid, so…she wasn't the happiest that I didn't tell her, but she said she was glad you had someone to hang out with after seeing the turnout. And she wants you to have a good time."

"That's why she's staring at you like you're on the naughty list?"

So, he was right. Stella was watching his every move. "She's staring at us because she's worried that you're worrying, and everyone knows two worries cancel each other out. It's science."

Willa's brow scrunched. "That doesn't make any sense."

"Of course it does. I learned it in college." Liam picked up his donut, took a bite, and continued between chewing. "But if you don't start enjoying this, we're going to be in big trouble."

It was the longest twenty minutes of Liam's life. Never in his thirty-five years had it taken so much energy to smile through a simple breakfast. Nor had he ever felt so relieved to have a teacher show up.

With Willa's class lining up to leave, Liam waved goodbye and headed for the exit. He'd barely stepped through the doors into the hall when he spotted Stella coming from the bathroom. "Can we talk?"

"You have some nerve." Stella sneered.

"Look, I should have told you, I get that, but I had already told her I would come, and I couldn't take it back."

"You mean, you told her you would come after I explicitly told you not to?" Stella crossed her arms and shifted her weight to one hip.

Liam rubbed the back of his neck where the tension was building. "I saw her sitting down there on the dock, and I wanted to make sure she was okay. The words were out of my mouth before I knew what I was saying. I wasn't trying to undermine you, I just…"

"You just told my daughter it was okay to lie to her mother. You're practically a stranger to her, and you're getting her to keep your secrets for you. Do you get how dangerous that is?"

Her words were a punch in the gut. When she said it out loud like that he felt like a creep. If he found out some guy was doing that to his niece, he'd string the fucker up by his balls. But Willa didn't feel like a stranger to him. Odd as it might sound, in the few short weeks he'd known her, Willa felt like a part of his life. Maybe he was projecting his feelings for Stella onto her daughter, but she was important to him.

Liam hung his head in shame. "I didn't think about it like that."

"Of course you didn't, because you're not her father. This isn't some game you can play."

"Stella, I'm not trying to play any game. I told you I was here for you, but you're so hell-bent on pushing me away that you can't stop to think that maybe I'm telling the truth." Frustration climbed his spine and settled at the base of his neck. It was always the same argument.

"It doesn't matter because here I thought you had changed, and it turns out you're still the guy who says one thing and does another."

His frustration curled into a tight ball. He hadn't actually gone back on his word. She'd told him not to come, but before he could argue his case, their conversation had turned into another fight about what he'd done twelve years ago. "For the record, you said it was best if I said I was busy, but I never got the chance to agree or disagree before you launched into your tirade about how you're so convinced I'm going to screw you over again."

"So now we're rationalizing our choice to be an asshole, and here I thought we'd moved on."

Fury soared through his veins. "Oh, cut the shit, Stella. You haven't moved on from anything. We both know you were never going to really forgive me. I was just a little slow figuring it out, but I'm done with this worn-out line dance we've been doing."

"Excuse me? And what worn-out line dance would that be?"

"The one where every time I take a step forward, you're taking two steps back. You've had your laces strapped ready to run from the moment you saw me."

"With good reason it seems."

Liam scrubbed a hand through his hair. "You know what, I was trying to apologize, but the truth is, I'm not sorry. And if you would open your damn eyes for one second, you'd see the truth. All I was trying to do was make that girl feel one less ounce of the disappointment and abandonment you're hell-bent on not letting go of. If for one minute, of one day, she didn't have to feel that kind of pain, then it was worth it. That kid deserves the world, but she also deserves a dad who is there for all the little moments."

"Miss James, is everything okay?"

He and Stella turned in unison to find Willa and her teacher standing in the hallway.

Shit, Willa was staring him down, tears building in her little eyes. Regret filled his soul. He should have waited to have it out with Stella when there were no young ears around to hear the truth. He should have kept his damn mouth shut about her father. Whatever Willa's relationship was with her dad, it wasn't his place to open his trap about it. Especially with her in earshot.

"Everything is fine." Stella's lips turned up into her weak but signature smile.

There was a good chance what he was about to do was going to push Stella over the edge, but seeing the pain in Willa's eyes, he didn't care. Liam took a few steps forward and knelt down in front of Willa. "Hey kiddo. Listen, I'm not sure how much I'm going to see you around, but I wanted to say thank you for inviting me today. You're a pretty cool kid to hang out with, so I'm honored that you wanted me to be here. And I want you to do me a favor, okay?"

Willa sniffled. "Okay."

"I want you to be good for your mom. This is just grown-up stuff, and sometimes it gets complicated, but none of that is on you, all right?"

Willa's arms flung around his neck, as a crack split across his chest. He was going to miss this kid more than he ever thought possible. She'd wormed her way into his heart without him even realizing it was happening.

"Time for me to go. Take care, Willa from Pebble Creek."

A slight smile tugged at her lips. "You too, Liam from Colorado."

Chapter Nineteen

The view outside Stella's office window was feeling a lot like her mood. The sky was smeared with dark gray clouds as the rain poured down in sheets. What should have been one of the most exciting days of her career was drowning in the relentless rain and her bleeding heart.

Stacy and her team from the network were scheduled to arrive at any moment—if they didn't float away first—and all Stella could think about was the disaster the week had been. If she'd told Willa once, she'd told her a hundred times, the mess with Liam wasn't her fault. The problem was, Stella was having a hard time remembering who was actually at fault. She had every right to be mad at Liam for withholding the truth, and she was, but she couldn't escape the nagging feeling that maybe she was more to blame than anyone.

His words had struck a chord.

And the thing that bothered her the most was the thing he was most right about. She'd been so focused on waiting for him to screw her over that she hadn't seen what he was doing for Willa. He'd never planned for Stella to find out, which meant it had nothing to do with gaining her favor, and everything to do with not wanting Willa to feel alone or abandoned.

"Any sign of them yet?"

Stella turned to find Whitney walking through her office door. "No, but I can hardly see up the driveway in this rain. I couldn't have ordered a worse day to showcase the place to a freaking TV network if I tried. I'm just hoping the rain slows up soon so we can walk the grounds."

"You should probably be hoping you find your good sense and better attitude, too."

Stella's mouth fell open. "Excuse me!"

"All I'm saying is this is a huge opportunity. I hope your head is in the right place." Whitney shrugged as though her words hadn't jabbed Stella in the gut.

"Thanks for the vote of confidence."

"I know you've had a lot going on this week, but this is some serious door opening stuff."

"You think I don't know that?" The pressure building at the base of Stella's skull was going to explode at any moment. This could mean huge things for her business. Free press for starters. Plus, all the people who would want to visit the place Sawyer Linden stayed while filming the special. It could really open them up to a larger market. "I'm sorry, I don't mean to take any of this out on you. I'm worried about Wil, and trying to focus on this meeting at the same time."

"She'll come around." Whitney's lips turned up in a gentle smile. "And besides, rain is supposed to be good luck."

"I think that only applies to weddings." The quiet laughter that rose up from Stella's chest was a welcome relief.

"Hey, we do weddings, so it's kind of the same thing."

Stella smiled at her best friend. "When I grow up, I want to be an optimist like you."

"I teach a class on Saturday mornings, if you're interested." Whitney winked. "Come on, this is going to be great. Like a new beginning. Out with the old and in with the new, right?"

"Right." Stella glanced out the window in time to see the SUV pulling down the drive. "Well, here goes nothing."

For an hour, Stella and Whitney sat across the table from the production crew and listened to all of their plans. It was amazing how much work went into planning a show like this. Even the little things were taken in to account. Things in the background Stella had never paid attention to when watching a reality show, but now she would.

When the rain let up, Stella took the opportunity to lead the group outside. As they walked around the grounds, notes were made and questions were asked. It was all overwhelming, but as far as she could tell, Stacy and her crew seemed pleased with what they saw.

"I think I've seen everything I need to see today." Stacy took one last look around the gardens. "I know we've taken up a fair amount of your day, but I like what I see. If you have a little more time, I'd like to go back inside and discuss the particulars."

Stella glanced at her watch and then at Whitney. "Could you grab Willa from school?"

"Absolutely," Whitney agreed and excused herself from the group.

"Let's head back into the conference room." Stella led the group back inside and down the grand hallway.

As they gathered around the table, Stacy glanced at her crew, seeming to get a silent confirmation they were all on the same page. "Stella, you have a beautiful place here, and based on what I've seen, I have no doubt you stay very busy, but I think I speak for everyone when I say this place would be perfect."

"Wow! Thank you." Stella's heart swelled in her chest. She'd always loved the way Pebble Creek turned out, but it felt good to hear it from a TV producer.

"I'd like to spend most of October and maybe the first week or so of November filming. I understand it's a lot to ask only six months out, and as I stated over the phone we will compensate very well, but is there any chance you could make it work on your end?"

Stella opened the case on her iPad and took a look at the schedule. Things were definitely slower just before the holidays. The calm before the storm. Most of her bookings for retreats and family reunions were in the summer months when her guests could enjoy the outdoor activities. "I have two weddings in October, one the first weekend and the other the third weekend. And then I have a group of writers coming for a retreat the second weekend in November."

"I think we can work around those." Stacy was swiping through her phone. "We can plan to start after the first wedding, and I can send most of the crew back to Atlanta for the weekend while you're dealing with the second wedding. If all goes well, we would be wrapped before your writers group arrives. If not, I can always move the remaining crew to Carefree. It should be finishing touches at that point."

With that, Stacy gave her crew a look that obviously said their work here was done, because they stood and shook hands with Stella before grabbing their things.

Stella followed Stacy to the door and stopped on the front porch.

"I'll be in touch as soon as we get all the details worked out, but I'm excited my assistant found this place. I think it's going to work out well."

Stella couldn't help the laughter that bubbled up. When Stacy gave her a curious look, she explained, "Sorry. This is probably too much information, but my life has been a bit complicated the past few weeks. I guess I just expected this to follow suit, but it went way smoother than I ever imagined."

Stacy nodded her head in understanding. "I know people in this industry get a bad rep for being bossy and demanding, but that's not my style. I want the people I work with to enjoy the experience. And since we're over sharing," Stacy winked, "for Sawyer's sake, we have to make this work. She's getting hammered in the media with the divorce, and if I want a job, I've gotta pull a rabbit out of my hat. We may need to do some promo stuff before October to start teasing the special, but that will all take place at the inn, so we won't be in your hair until the fall. And Stella…"

"Yeah?" Stella sensed the change in Stacy's tone.

"I hope things get better for you. You've got a good thing going here. Hold on to that."

On the bright side, at least Stella didn't have a media storm blasting her personal problems to the world.

*****

For the fourth night in a row, Liam sat on one of his sibling's couches with a cold beer in his hand. Tonight, he'd taken up residence at Drew's, given he'd spent the past two evenings at Carter's house, and the afternoon before that at Miles and Julia's. Tomorrow, he and the brothers were taking the boat out fishing and Sunday would be dinner at his parents' house.

After that, he wasn't sure what he was doing with his life.

Since shit had gone south with Stella, he had more free time than he was comfortable with. It was time to figure out what came next now that he was permanently back in Carefree.

As though Drew was reading his mind, his brother cleared his throat. "Don't take this the wrong way, because I'm glad you're back in town, but what's your plan?"

"Right now? To sit here and drink this beer and then go get something to eat. Unless you're cooking for me?" Liam turned his bottle up for show.

"I meant more in the long-term sense. I'm assuming your gig with Stella is up, so what's next?"

Yeah, he was assuming the same thing. There was a small part of him that hated to leave Stella and Whitney in the lurch because he was a man of his word, but after everything that had gone down, there was no place for him there. He was finally closing that part of his life.

"I don't know, but I've gotta figure something out. This sitting around on my ass isn't cutting it, and there's no way I'm helping out at the diner again. That shit about killed me after one day, and I smelled like fried chicken for a week."

"You know, I've been short a few guys for a while. If you want, you can come out to the job site Monday, and sling a hammer around. If nothing else, you can get some of your pent-up frustration out until you figure out what's next."

"For sake of stating the obvious, you know I've only done renovation work, not straight up building from scratch, right?"

"Trust me, you wouldn't be the first guy to show up without any real experience." Drew let out a hearty laugh. "As long as you can hold a power tool and not kill anyone while you're there, my foreman can teach you the rest."

Drew's offer was tempting. Liam didn't know anything about building houses from the ground up, but he had learned a lot over the four months it took him to renovate his place in Colorado. If he could handle the finishing touches, surely, he could handle some instructions from a foreman. And banging the crap out of some nails sounded like a good way to get out some of the tension resting on his shoulders.

"I can definitely hold a power tool, and I managed not to kill any of my employees before, so I think we're good there." Hell, the fact that he hadn't killed Stella made him a damn saint.

Drew picked up his beer and raised it into the air. "Cheers to not having to bury dead bodies. Lord knows I've thought about it a time or two. Anyway, you're welcome to come help out as long as you want, and I might even throw you a dollar or two."

"How kind of you." Liam laughed.

"Kindness is my middle name." Drew took a drink of his beer. "Seriously, I could use the extra hands, so the door is open as long as you don't mind working for your baby bro. Now, onto more important things. What are you going to do about Stella?"

The sound of her name on Drew's lips was a punch in the gut. Despite all of his anger, he missed her, and quite possibly, he missed Willa more, but there was nothing he could do. Some things weren't meant to be.

Liam let out an exacerbated sigh. "Nothing."

"Did you try to apologize?"

He couldn't believe his brother was questioning him. "Are you kidding me? All I've done since I got back is apologize."

Drew held up his hands as a show of surrender. "I'm just checking. The men in this family can be a bit bullheaded, myself included. Hell, look at Miles. He had to fly to South America to get Julia to forgive his sorry ass. Good thing too, that woman is like the pot of gold at the end of a rainbow."

"You do realize she's married to our brother?" Liam shook his head.

"I know, but it didn't stop me from asking if she had a sister or a close cousin."

"I'm happy for them, but the only grand gesture Stella cares about is the one where I left and moved halfway across the country. Like Dad used to always say, you can beat a dead horse but it won't make it get back up and run."

"I don't know if I would call it a grand gesture, but you definitely made one hell of a move. None of us saw that one coming."

"Yeah, well the thing is, I'm not sorry for leaving. Maybe I went about it the wrong way, and I don't even blame her for being pissed, but honestly, I think it was for the best. If we would have gotten married back then, I'm pretty sure I would have been a shit husband. I was just a kid, that didn't know the first thing about being an adult. And when I look at Willa, I can't help but think shit happens for a reason. I know it's not how Stella planned for it to be, but I can't imagine this world without that kid. She's going to do something great. I know it."

Drew cocked his head. "That's a pretty strong statement."

"If you spent any amount of time with Willa, you'd get it. It's not just that she's wise beyond her years. She's awesome in so many ways."

"I'm sure she is, but I meant how you feel about her. It's like you already took that kid in and made her your own."

The thought rippled through Liam's chest. Most men wouldn't want to take on someone else's kid, but Liam would have accepted her as his own. Hell, Stella was worried about Willa getting attached to him, but the truth was, he was the one attached to Willa. Nine-years-old and that kid had wedged herself into his heart.

He and Stella had history, but there was something about Willa that had lit a fire in his heart. He'd never really given much thought to having kids, but the thought of not spending time with her hurt like hell.

Liam shook his head. He was letting his emotions get the best of him. He barely knew the kid, and yet he was acting like someone was taking away his prized possession.

"She's a cool kid, that's all." Liam waved off his emotions. It didn't matter what he thought anymore, that ship had more than sailed, it was resting on the bottom of the damn ocean.

Chapter Twenty

Normally by Friday, Stella would appreciate a quiet house, but considering the past few days, it was too quiet. Willa hadn't been herself since the incident at the school, and it was weighing on Stella. She wanted to assure her daughter that things would go back to normal. She just wasn't sure what normal was anymore.

Everything felt different.

Walking through the house, Stella popped her head into Willa's room and was surprised to find it empty. Her daughter always retreated to her bedroom when she wasn't happy about something. Stella stood motionless and listened for the tiniest sound, but the house was quiet as a mouse.

Moving across the hall, she stepped into the master bedroom and glanced around, but her daughter was nowhere in sight. And then she heard it. The tiny rustle coming from her walk-in closet.

Stella spoke softly as she took in the scene on her closet floor. "What are you doing in here?"

Her daughter was sitting in the middle of the small space, a box open in front of her. All around her were photos and old mementos. It was the box Stella had held onto for far too long. A box full of her life with Liam.

Startled by her presence, Willa rushed to return the items to the box.

"I'm sorry." Willa's voice was soft as she kept her eyes averted.

"It's okay." Stella took a seat on the floor next to her daughter. "There's a lot of old stuff in that box."

Picking up a photo, she stared at the younger version of herself. The girl in the photo was full of wonder, not yet fully jaded by the world around her. What she wouldn't give to be that young and full of hope again.

"I know you're mad."

Stella hated how weak and defeated her daughter's words sounded. It was very unlike the child who was so confident and sure of herself.

"You're wrong, you know." Stella rubbed a gentle hand down her daughter's hair. "I'm not mad. You're curious and I get that. I was curious at your age, too."

"It's not the first time I saw it." Willa glanced up with a sadness in her eyes.

The words took Stella by surprise. Willa had never mentioned anything about it, which was odd. Her perceptive nature always had her asking questions. "When did you find it?"

Willa was quiet for a long moment. "The day before we met Liam at the diner. I was playing dress up, and I was looking for those red shoes you never wear anymore. I accidently knocked the box off the top shelf, and the stuff fell out."

A million thoughts raced through Stella's mind, but she kept landing on the same question. "Why didn't you say something?"

Willa shrugged her slender shoulders. "It didn't seem important."

Stella knew better. As smart as her daughter was, she was a terrible liar. "You mean, you didn't want to get in trouble?"

"That too." They sat in silence, staring at the photos for a long moment before Willa spoke again. "Then we saw him at the diner. I recognized him from the photos, and you two were acting like the people in those movies you and Aunt Whit always watch. I thought if he filled in for Jackson, maybe you would get back together. Like they do in the movies."

Stella was astounded by the words coming out of her daughter's mouth. "Baby, movies aren't real, and life is more complicated."

"I know...that's what Liam said too."

A swell of emotion rolled through her. "What exactly did Liam say?"

"That he made some really dumb mistakes, and you have a hard time trusting him now. But I thought if I kept inviting him to things, you would trust him again. Like after I invited him to my party, we went to lunch, and then to his parents' house. I thought if I invited him to school, you would see he's a good guy, but I made the dumb mistake this time. I messed it all up."

The sadness in her daughter's eyes broke Stella's heart. "Oh, sweet girl, you didn't mess anything up. There's just a lot of history between Liam and me."

"But you love each other, and he's gone all because of me. If I wouldn't have invited him, you wouldn't have gotten mad, and he wouldn't have left. It's all my fault." Tears welled, as her voice faltered.

How did Stella explain to her nine-year-old that Liam left because she couldn't get over herself? How did she explain she'd hung on to the resentment so long it had hardened her heart, without risking her daughter doing the same thing? Stella had built the walls so high it was impossible for anyone to climb over them. Liam had done nothing but try to prove he was sorry for the way things ended, and yet she couldn't accept it because the truth was she was still stuck in the same place from twelve years ago.

Before Stella could put a coherent sentence together, Willa lifted up a tiny, black velvet box. "You were supposed to marry Liam, weren't you?"

Stella stared at the box as reality dawned like a new day. She'd spent years casting the blame of their failed engagement all on Liam, but now that her daughter was looking to her for the truth, she couldn't lie to herself any longer.

Their demise had been a two-way street.

It was so clear now. She'd pushed Liam to propose because in some messed up way, she thought it would make him stay. But her father had more legal responsibility to stay, and he'd still left. Why she'd thought forcing Liam to marry her would make him stay any more than her father had been a fool's errand.

In truth, she hadn't been any more ready to walk down the aisle than Liam. All her pushing had done was push them further apart. The same way she was pushing them apart now. She hadn't fought for him then, nor was she fighting for him now.

History couldn't repeat itself.

Stella jumped up from her place on the floor as though the truth were lighting a literal fire under her ass. She had to make things right. Liam was brave enough to admit he'd never gotten over her. It was time for her to step out in faith.

Grabbing a pair of shoes from the bottom rack, Stella quickly slipped them onto her feet.

"Mom, what are you doing?" Willa glanced up at her in total confusion.

Right, she needed to do this without an audience. "I need to take care of something. I'm going to drop you off at Grandma's for a little while."

A bright smile spread across Willa's lips. "You're going to get him back."

"I'm going to try."

*****

"What are you two doing here?" The familiar sound of Kat's bossy voice caught Liam's attention as he walked through the front door of the diner.

"Us? What are you doing here? Aren't you supposed to be on maternity leave or something?"

Myriad emotions passed over his sister's face as he and Drew approached the bar. Kat had always been a strong, independent woman, and the diner had been the center of her world for a long time. He wasn't surprised she couldn't stay away.

"I needed a breather. I feel like all I am is a milk factory these days." Kat grabbed her chest for emphasis.

A guttural gag escaped Drew's mouth. "Dude, TMI."

"I know it's probably hard to believe, but your sister has boobs. And they make milk. It's kind of their whole purpose," Kat shot back.

This is exactly why Liam had come home. Well, not to talk about his sister's boobs, but he missed the banter, the sibling fights, but most of all being able to see them whenever he wanted to. How many years had he missed out on moments like this? Just a random run in on a Friday night.

Liam glanced over the counter. "Where is the rugrat anyway?"

"At home with her capable father, hence the breather part." Kat's face had *Duh* written all over it. "So, is this what a wild night for two bachelors looks like? Eating at my diner?"

"It's not like we live in a metropolis," Drew jabbed back. "Not a lot of options."

"Thanks, Dipshit." Kat grabbed a menu from behind the counter. "Just for that, you're ordering off the menu. No special treatment."

"Oh com'on," Drew whined.

Without another word, Kat walked away and started talking with other customers in the diner. Liam watched as they smiled and congratulated her on the baby. It was nice to see two of his siblings getting the life they wanted. Miles and Julia were living in their newly wed bliss, and Kat had a husband and daughter. Liam wasn't sure what life held for him, but the idea of dating in his thirties sounded like a cruel form of torture. Maybe he would just be the cool uncle who got to do all the fun things without all the work.

Beside him, Drew stood up from his stool and walked around the end of the counter to make himself a drink. "I still can't believe our sister was hooking up with Brooks." Drew shook his head as a shiver ran through his shoulders.

"Pretty sure she's still hooking up with him since they're married." Liam laughed when his brother made a disgusted face.

"Dude, that is not the mental image I need. You don't find it a little bit weird?"

"I don't know." Liam glanced at his sister and then back to Drew. "It kind of makes sense. Brooks always felt like part of the family, now it's official. And he's sure as shit better than her ex."

"You know he's running for Governor in Georgia, right?" Drew slid a glass of sweet tea across the counter to him.

"I heard. Can't say I'm surprised, the preppy douchebag, but I'd take Brooks over that piece of shit any day of the week."

"That we can agree on, Brother. Now, we need to agree on you fixing this thing with Stella."

The pit in Liam's gut opened up. Why the hell couldn't his brother let it go? "Drop it. I told you I'm done with that shit. Leave it alone.

"What's done?" He hadn't heard Kat approaching.

Liam took a deep breath. He'd purposely been avoiding Kat all week because she was a meddler, and a fixer. He had no doubt she knew about the drama with Stella. Kat always knew everything. But he didn't want her getting involved. She already thought she was some kind of cupid.

"Nothing." Liam groaned.

"Our dear brother made of mess of things with Stella and doesn't want to fix it."

That was it. Liam was taking back every nice thing he'd said about being home. He was moving to Alaska where his nosy siblings couldn't be all up in his non-existent love life. Things were over with him and Stella. Everyone just needed to accept it.

"We've been over this. I spent the past few weeks trying to make things right, but she's not interested, so it's over."

Kat's cellphone dinged at an incoming text. Liam watched as she pulled it from her back pocket and read the message. A bright smile spread across her lips. "I don't know. Sometimes people surprise you."

"Don't even think about it. I see your wheels turning," Liam warned.

"My wheels aren't turning." Kat laughed. "I'm just texting my husband that I was here with you and Drew."

She was up to something, but Liam couldn't quite tell what. He'd seen that face before. It was the face she always made when she was formulating one of her master plans. "I'm warning you, Kat, do not get involved. You'll only make it worse."

"I'm not doing anything." Kat held her phone up to Drew. "Tell him I'm texting Brooks."

Drew read the message on her phone, and a smile spread across his lips. "She's not lying. It's just Brooks."

"Fine, let me see it then."

Kat scoffed and tucked her phone in her back pocket. "If you don't trust us, that's a *you* problem. Now, what do you want to eat?"

"Allison Katherine Brooks, I swear to you…"

"Geez, are you my mother now? Are you going to ground me?" Kat snapped back.

"Dude, calm down. It really was just Brooks."

Liam didn't trust his siblings as far as he could throw them. They were up to something. He could feel it, but he couldn't deal with them on an empty stomach. He would eat, and then he would deal with whatever it was they were up to.

Chapter Twenty-One

Stella wasn't one to put herself out there. Not like this. She liked her tidy little box where everything was controlled. But when it came to Liam, she'd never felt more out of control in her life.

The night air, blowing in through her open car window, was cool against Stella's heated skin as she made the drive into Carefree. Above, tiny glimpses of moonlight fought to break through the growing clouds. There was a storm brewing, she could feel the thickness as the humidity hung heavy in the air.

Turning on to Liam's street, she gripped the steering wheel as a replay of their fight rolled through her mind. She'd been awful. Probably not as awful as she would have been if they hadn't been standing in the hallway of Willa's school, but still, she'd said things she couldn't take back. She'd all but called him a creep and a liar, and made him out to be a monster, when all he was trying to do was support Willa.

Regret was a terrible emotion.

Stella parked her car on the street, the same as she'd done the first night she'd come here. So many things had been said that night, so many confessions. His honesty and openness had planted a seed of fear in her heart. As much as she wanted to believe his words, she'd been terrified, but the idea of losing him again scared her more.

Liam coming home was a second chance. A chance, she realized now, she didn't want to throw away.

Stepping from her car, Stella made her way up the driveway, her heart dropping at the absence of Liam's truck. What if he had already decided to move on? Was he out on a date? It was Friday night, and he was a grown man with needs. It wouldn't be a complete shock if he'd taken someone up on an offer.

Her mind flashed back to Sherri and her vulturous circling. A woman like that was persistent in her endeavors. Stella should have never told Sherri he was single and wealthy. She wouldn't be surprised if the woman had tracked him down.

All she could manage to do was stand in the middle of the driveway, staring at the empty spot where his truck had once sat. She should have called, at the very least texted him, but she'd been so set on making amends she'd never imagined him being anywhere but home.

Now her imagination was running wild.

"Can I help you with something?"

Stella spun, startled by the deep voice coming from Kat's porch. In the dim light, she could just make out the shape of Brooks sitting in the rocking chair, a tiny infant pressed to his chest.

"Oh wow. You scared me. I didn't see you sitting there." Stella took a few steps across the gravel toward the open porch as her heart pounded in her chest.

"Sorry, that wasn't my intention, but then again, I didn't intend to have a woman standing in the middle of my driveway either." Brooks' phone lit up then, casting a soft glow around him and the baby. After a few seconds the glow disappeared, and Brooks stood from his seat. "I don't know what it is about the night air, but it's the only thing that makes her happy."

Stella climbed the few steps to the porch. She was already trespassing, no need to be rude. "I remember those days. I used to get annoyed when people would say *'you'll miss it when they're grown'* when I felt like I was in the fight of my life, but then I blinked, and somehow Willa is nine."

"I obviously only met her the one-time last Sunday, but it seems like you did a pretty good job with her. Got any pointers?" Brooks let out a soft chuckle.

"Honestly, I think I got lucky."

From his pocket, Brooks' phone let out another soft ding. "You mind holding her for a second?"

"Absolutely not, I would love to." Stella lifted her hands and took the sleeping child from her father. She was more than happy to hold her as long as he needed. She missed the baby snuggles more than anything.

Brooks typed out a response before slipping the phone back in his pocket. "Thanks. Kat said she needed to go to the diner to *check on things,*" Brooks air quoted the words as he spoke them, "but I think she needed a little break. Of course, that doesn't mean she isn't texting me every five minutes to make sure I haven't broken the baby." He let out a soft laugh.

Stella glanced down to the squishy bundle in her arms. "Do you mind if I hold her for a few more minutes. I miss this part."

"Be my guest." Brooks gestured to the rocking chairs. "You can come by every evening and hold her all you want."

Stella took a seat as lightening lit up in the distance followed by rolling thunder. It had been years since she'd spent time with Brooks, but he was just as mellow as always. Any time she and Liam had come home to visit, Brooks had always been around. She'd come to think of him as just another brother. It was nice to see that he was truly a part of the family now.

"I used to tell Liam that you and Kat would end up together, but he said I was crazy. Guess I was right." Stella smiled up at the new dad.

"Yeah, well, I wasn't so sure last year." Brooks paused for a moment before continuing. "I'm not trying to pry or anything, but I heard Kat and Julia talking about you two the other day. I love the Scott family like my own, always have, but they can be a bit difficult to manage sometimes. I'm not saying what Liam did was right, I probably would have killed the man if it were my daughter, but he means well. Sometimes they go about things the hard way. Trust me, Kat did some shi—stuff that made me want to wring her neck, but we got past it and look at us now."

Stella watched as the man next to her smiled down at his daughter with pure love. There was so much admiration, tears welled in her eyes.

"That's actually why I was hoping to talk to him tonight, but I guess he's not home." Stella glanced toward the apartment above the detached garage. "It took me some time to see the truth, but I get that he was just trying to be there for Willa. I may have overreacted a tiny bit."

"It happens to the best of us. I accused Kat of using me as a sperm donor when she turned down my proposal, so I'm well versed on overreacting."

In the dim light, she could still make out the look of regret written on his face. "You didn't."

"Oh, I did." Brooks sighed. *"Definitely not* my shining moment, but I was hurt, and the words kind of flew out there."

"Yeah, I know the feeling." Stella fought the memories from replaying again. "I guess I'm not the only one who says things they wish they could take back."

"At least, you figured out it's never too late to try."

"You obviously figured it out." Stella glanced down as Penelope squirmed.

"No, but thankfully Kat did. I'm not sure where we would be if she hadn't made me get over myself. Not that I mind the company, but I feel like I should tell you he's at the diner with Kat."

Relief washed over Stella. The baby had been a good distraction, but in the back of her mind, she hadn't stopped wondering if he was out on a date with someone else. Before she could respond, lightening lit up the night sky all around them.

"I should probably get her back inside. I doubt getting struck by lightning will instill trust in my wife."

Standing, Stella handed the baby back to Brooks. "Thanks for the chat. It actually helped a lot."

"Anytime. I don't really have much of a social life anymore." Brooks laughed as he headed for the door.

Crossing the yard, Stella felt the first few drops fall from the sky. The storm was rolling in quick, and if she didn't want to get soaked, she needed to hurry.

The drive across town took an eternity. At least, it felt like it every time she got stopped by a red light. The light rain was beginning to pick up as she turned onto Main Street, but she could see the diner in the distance. She just needed to make it fifty yards before the bottom fell out.

Pulling into a spot next to the front of the building, Stella stepped out of her car in time to watch Liam, Drew, and Kat exit the diner. His cold, hard stare locked on her the moment he looked up. She'd been so focused on her personal revelation, she'd never stopped to wonder if he would want to see her. She'd assumed he would be happy, but based on the death stare he was giving her across the pavement, she'd assumed wrong.

"What are you doing here?" His words were as icy as his eyes.

In that instance, every word she'd rehearsed on the way vanished from her brain. Her mind was like a blank canvas, void of any content. There were so many things she wanted to tell him, and yet not one thing would come to mind. All she could focus on was the sea of regret between them.

Just then, the sky flashed bright as dawn, and thunder cracked all around them. Rain poured down from the heavens as she was transported back to the night in the boat house. He'd stood motionless in the window as the rain fell in droves outside. Maybe it had been the wine or the years of longing for him, but she hadn't held back. She dove in head first.

"I was as much to blame as you."

Chapter Twenty-Two

Liam stood under the eve of the diner as the rain began to pour down. Maybe he was delusional from not sleeping well, but he could have sworn Stella had said she was as much to blame as he was. The only problem, he wasn't sure which thing she was referring to. The list of things she blamed him for grew by the day.

Either way, it was the first time she'd ever taken any accountability for their problems.

The anger that had been festering for days wanted to leave her out there in the rain like the fool he felt, but his father hadn't raised him to be a jackass.

"Come inside and we'll talk." Liam bellowed over the loud roar of the rain hitting the metal roof of the diner.

"No."

The word struck him. He knew she was stubborn, but damn. She was standing there getting drenched, and yet she wasn't willing to come inside.

He shouldn't be surprised. "No, you don't want to come inside, or no you don't want to talk?"

The desire to leave her standing there with her ass in her hand was growing by the second, but somewhere in the dark depths of his soul, he wanted to know what she meant. Maybe it was morbid curiosity or maybe he was just a fool, but he'd waited a long time to hear her say she was to blame for anything.

"No, I have to say this now." She glanced around as though she were noticing the rain for the first time.

"Fine, but I'm not coming out there." He was done trying to meet her halfway. If she had something to say, she was going to have to come to him. He'd bent over backward, more than an Olympic gymnast.

As Stella started to approach, he heard Kat's hushed voice over his shoulder. "This is going to be good."

Liam spun around to meet his sister's eyes. She and Drew were a few paces behind, eyes wide with wonder. "Do you mind?"

"I kind of do." Kat smirked. "It is my place of business after all."

"Seriously?" Liam cut his eyes and cocked his head.

"Oh, come on. I haven't been out of my house in weeks," Kat whined. "I need some excitement in my life."

Drew wrapped his arm around their sister and shot Liam a wink. "I'll catch a ride back with Kat to her house. You can bring the truck when you're done."

"Party pooper." Kat called as they walked around the end of the building toward her car.

Once his siblings were out of sight, he turned his focus back to Stella. In the short time she'd stood in the parking lot, the rain had soaked through her sweatshirt. The gentleman in him wished he had something dry to offer her, but he hadn't been prepared for rain either. The storm had blown in out of nowhere.

"You were saying..." He clung to his patience, but he was losing the battle.

Her chest rose with a deep inhale. "I couldn't find Willa."

All the frustration and anger drained from his body in an instant. If anything had happened to Willa, so help him God. "Is she okay?"

"Oh! No, she's fine. I meant she wasn't in her room when I went to get her."

The sudden adrenaline spike started to wane. For a split second, he thought something terrible had happened.

"Anyway, that's not the point," Stella continued. "When I found her, she was in my closet going through a box of some old stuff. Photos mostly. Turns out, it wasn't the first time. I guess she found it the day before we saw you here at the diner. She knew you were the guy from the photos in the box."

Liam wasn't interested in a walk down memory lane. He wanted to get back to the part where she was actually taking some responsibility for their issues.

234

"Okay? So, what do old photos and her knowing who I was have to do with you being just as much to blame?"

"Willa said you told her you made some dumb mistakes in the past and I didn't trust you anymore." Her words drifted as though she was waiting for him to confirm.

It felt like a trap. Another thing for her to disapprove of, but at this point what did it matter. "I don't remember the exact words, but that's more or less the gist."

"The thing is, I made some mistakes, too. I pushed you into proposing when neither one of us were ready. I thought in some messed up way that if we got married, you wouldn't leave like my father did, but instead, all my pushing did was make you want to leave."

How long had he wanted to hear her say those words? For her to take any responsibility in what had happened? Yes, he had ultimately been the one to leave, but things had been rocky for a while. He'd seen the fracture splitting between them. In some ways, maybe it was the reason he started looking for a job in another city.

For twelve years, he'd wanted this kind of validation that he hadn't been the only one to blame, but he couldn't help but feel nostalgia was driving her thoughts. "And what happens when this sentimental moment wears off?"

He hated to be this way, it wasn't in his nature, but they had been down this path before. They'd shared a very nostalgic moment the night of Miles's wedding, and look where that had led them. He couldn't keep doing this back-and-forth thing with her. As much as he wanted her, a few old photos in a box didn't change a person.

"That's not what this is." Stella whispered.

"A week ago, you were certain I would change my mind about wanting kids of my own. Realizing you were part of the problem in the past doesn't change the present." He needed to be certain she meant what she said.

"I was scared to let you in. I was looking for any excuse to make things not work, but...I realized I was wrong."

"And if I want kids?"

*****

The wet cotton of her sweatshirt clung to Stella as she stood motionless, letting his words sink in. He didn't trust her. Not that she could blame him. Her own emotions over the past few weeks had given her whiplash.

Her thoughts drifted to his niece nestled in her arms. The sweet scent of Penelope's tiny head as she slept soundly against Stella's chest. Just the thought of holding her precious life in her hands had brought joy to Stella's heart in the midst of a rugged week.

Could she give that to Liam? Could she start over if that's what his heart desired?

She'd lost so much time with him already, but the idea of missing another moment made anything seem possible. "If that's something you really want, then I think we can discuss it."

The look of shock on his face said it all. He hadn't expected her to concede.

"Why?" Liam finally found his words. "Why now when you were so set against it?"

"I wish there was an answer that didn't point directly to selfishness, but there isn't one. The truth is, I don't know if I want any more kids. I gave up on the notion a long time ago. But what I do know is, I don't want to spend another moment of this life without you. I made a lot of mistakes, and I let you take the blame for a long time, but I'd be a fool to not realize the biggest mistake of my life is letting you walk away."

Once the words were flowing, she couldn't stop them. "I don't know if you want to make this work or maybe you're done with me, but I had to try. I never fought for us. I let you walk away, and I never tried to stop you. I spent years dwelling on everything that happened, but I never did anything to change it. I expected you to fail me, and so I willed it into fruition. I believed it into existence because that's all I knew. Men leave. I think deep down I was always waiting for it to happen. Then and now. But you're not my father."

Hot tears streaked across her cold, damp cheek. She needed him to know the truth. Even if it didn't change his mind, she couldn't walk away this time without telling him exactly how she felt.

"Stella—" He spoke her name softly.

Stella held up her hand, stopping him from speaking another word. "No, I need to say this." The way he spoke her name, so soft and apprehensive, whispered of regret. Regardless, she needed to finish before she lost her nerve. "From the moment you showed up at your brother's wedding, I knew I was still in love with you. I lied to you when I said I was trying to figure out who's phone was left."

"I'm aware." A gentle smile spread across his lips, but she ignored the tingle in her gut.

"When I realized the code was my birthday, I didn't know what to think. And then I found myself scrolling through your photos. I wanted to see if there was someone in your life. Part of me wished I would have found someone because it would have meant that you had moved on, and maybe I could finally move on too. But there wasn't anyone. Nor did you have a ring on your finger. And then the boat house happened."

The memories of their night together rolled through her mind like a silent film. "It was like we picked up right where we left off, which scared me more than anything. So much has happened since you left, but in some weird way, it didn't feel like it that night. I felt like I was in my twenties again. Then morning came. I knew what my heart wanted, but my head kept getting in the way. And then I saw you getting close to Willa. I know you never planned on me finding out about the whole school thing—"

"Stella, about that."

"No, that's the thing. You didn't plan on me finding out. You went because you care about her. You risked everything for her happiness. It's what any parent would do."

Disbelief colored his face. "What are you saying?"

"I'm saying I'm sorry. Look, I don't know if you really want kids of your own or if it was just some kind of test, but what I do know is there is a little girl who very much wants you in her life…"

Slipping her hand into her back pocket, Stella pulled out the black velvet box. "And so does her mom."

Chapter Twenty-Three

Liam's eyes locked on the small velvety box in Stella's hand as his brain tried to catch up with the turn of events. He recognized the case. It was the one he'd given her all those years ago. He could still remember the shape of the diamond. It wasn't much of a ring, but it was all he could afford back then. Not that he had really been able to afford it.

The memory of her smiling face the day he'd proposed was one he would never forget. She'd been so happy when he'd opened the box that all his fears had drifted away with the wind.

The ding of the diner door brought him back to the present. He'd been so lost in her words that he'd forgotten they were standing on the sidewalk outside of his sister's restaurant. Liam smiled politely as an older couple passed by, their curious gazes locked on Stella's hand. Were they wondering the same thing he was?

He waited for the couple to get into their car before he spoke. "Are you proposing to me?"

A crimson blush bloomed across her cheeks. "I don't really know. What would you say if I were?"

Her anxiety rolled off her in waves. "I would say I have a better idea for the ring that's in that box."

"Oh!"

It wasn't fair to her, but Liam couldn't hold in his laughter when she misunderstood what he meant. "That didn't come out like I meant it. I don't think the ring in that box is going to fit my finger. Hell, I'm not even sure it will fit you anymore, but I have a better idea."

"Okay." Her voice was full of hesitation.

"Do you trust me?" A plan was unfolding in his head, but he wasn't quite ready to share it yet.

"If you would have asked me two minutes ago, I would have said yes. Now? I feel like you're up to something."

Leaning in, Liam pressed a gentle kiss upon her lips. "I promise, it will be worth it." As he pulled back, he placed his hand around the tiny box. "But I'm going to need to hang on to this for the moment."

*****

Stella paced across her living room for the hundredth time since Liam had walked out the front door that morning.

Everything, from the moment they left the diner the night before until now felt like a blur. Somehow, they'd managed to keep their hands off each other long enough to return Drew's truck and make it back to her place. For a few blissful hours, they'd had the house to themselves before Stella's mom had returned Willa home.

Willa had been delighted to see Liam sitting on the couch when she'd walked through the front door. And for the first time in a long time, everything was right in Stella's world.

"You're pacing again, Mom." Willa called as she walked through the living room, heading for the kitchen.

She was. "I am not."

Her daughter's head popped back around the corner. "You totally are. Where did Liam go anyway?"

It was the question that had been weighing on Stella since the moment Drew had pulled in her driveway four hours ago. "He went to get his truck from his brother's house."

It was the only part of his plan he'd bothered to share with her, despite her constant questioning. The black box was nowhere to be found—not that she'd completely torn her room apart looking for it this morning. Even though she'd practically proposed to him the night before, she couldn't control the butterflies flapping in her stomach. She hated surprises.

Willa reappeared from the kitchen with a glass of orange juice in hand. "So, is Liam moving in now?"

The question took Stella by surprise. There hadn't been much conversing of any subject after Willa had gone to bed, much less where Liam would be spending his nights. Nor had she broached the subject with her daughter. "Well, we haven't discussed it. Does it bother you that Liam stayed here last night?"

"No, I was just curious." Willa shrugged as she took a seat on the couch. "What's for lunch?"

Stella wasn't sure what she expected, but the lack of concern wasn't it.

She was about to text Liam, to see if he was coming back in time to eat with them, when his truck pulled into the driveway. Glancing out the window, Stella took in the two large pizza boxes in his hand. "Looks like we're having pizza for lunch."

Willa spun on the couch, peered out the window like a puppy excited to see its owner, and then bolted for the door. Opening the storm door, she yelled, "Yes! You brought pizza."

"I figured since I was in town, I couldn't come back empty handed. You still like cheese, right?" Liam smiled at Stella as he moved through the living room into the kitchen, with Willa in tow.

"It's my favorite." Excitement filled her daughter's voice.

Stella followed the aroma into the kitchen. She hadn't realized how hungry she was until the smell of Italian seasonings filled her house. "Four hours to get your truck and pizza?" She shot Liam a questioning glance.

"And a shower." He winked.

So, he still wasn't telling her this master plan of his. She'd see about that. "No other stops?"

"Is your mom always this nosy?" Liam nudged Willa with his elbow and laughed.

"Always. She hates surprises." Willa's attention was focused fully on opening the box and grabbing the first slice of pizza.

"We have plates, you know." Stella sighed.

"But I'm starving." Willa raised the slice to her mouth.

Liam shrugged and cast an apologetic smile Stella's way. "I guess we're eating from the box."

She was in trouble, in more ways than one. These two together were going to be a force to be reckoned with. Their connection was already so strong. Grabbing a slice of her own, Stella sat back and watched her daughter and the man she loved bond over pizza crust. How had she gotten so lucky?

The journey had not been easy, but the risk had been worth the reward. There were a million things to figure out, but for the moment, all she wanted was to take it all in.

"I did make one other stop." Liam wiped his hands with a napkin before reaching into the side pocket of his cargo shorts. Turning his attention toward Willa, he produced a small jewelry box. "I have something for you, but before I give it to you, there's something I want to ask you."

"Okay." Willa glanced at the box, and then back to Liam, her interest peeked. "What is it?"

A smile spread across his face. "What's thirty-six divided by twelve?"

"Really?" Willa shook her head. "That's so easy."

——

244

"Well, what is it then, smarty pants?"

"It's three. Duh."

Raising a hand to her mouth, Stella's heart melted. It wasn't a simple math problem.

Willa's brow scrunched. "What am I missing?"

"Well," Liam smiled, "I'm *thirty-six,* and *twelve* years ago I made the mistake of leaving your mom behind, but if I hadn't then there wouldn't be the *three* of us now." Liam opened the box that now held a necklace. "Willa Ann James, would you make me the happiest man in the world, and let me be your bonus dad?"

Hot tears streaked across Stella's cheeks. She wasn't sure how he'd pulled it off in such a short amount of time, but the diamond he'd given her all those years ago was now nestled in a gold pendant, on a thin chain. It was absolutely perfect.

"Yes!" Willa's arms flung around his neck. "Yes! Yes! Yes!"

Liam pulled her daughter into his lap and hugged her tight. "What do you say we give your mom a gift, too?"

Willa pulled back with a bright smile on her face. "Does she get a necklace, too?"

"I have something a little better for her." Reaching into his pocket with a free hand, Liam pulled out a second box. "Stella James, for the sake of sticking with my cheesy math analogy, what do you say we stop with the division, and start doing some addition?"

With happy tears filling her eyes, Stella smiled. "I think addition sounds way easier."

Maybe it was true what they said, some things were worth the wait.

"Wait..." A bright grin spread across Willa's lips. "Does addition mean I get a baby brother or sister?"

THE END

Can't get enough of the Scott family? Keep reading for an excerpt from the Carefree Series, Book 4, coming soon.

Chapter One

Anxiety washed over Sawyer Linden as she slid her sunglasses in place and stepped out of her SUV. Instinctively, she lowered the brim of her hat until she could barely see beyond the edge. As far as the media was concerned, she was still in Atlanta, hiding out in her Candler Park townhouse. And the longer the world believed that, the better. But it was only a matter of time before someone recognized her.

The drive from Atlanta to Beaufort County, South Carolina had been the most uneventful four-and-a-half-hours of the past few months. A simple fact Sawyer was extremely grateful for. After the call she'd received the previous night, she'd needed the time to herself. Stacy, her long time show runner and creative director, had assured her they were working on replacing the general contractor, but it was just one more hit in a long list that never seemed to end. Shaun had been her contractor since the beginning of *Sweet Home Sawyer*, but she couldn't blame him for walking away.

Hell, she'd walk away from her life too if she could, but it wouldn't stop the media. Like a bad STD, it was the gift that kept on giving. Every time she thought things were beginning to die down, another ridiculous photo would grace the cover of the tabloids. At this rate, she deserved a trophy for the longest running gossip cycle.

Taking a deep breath, Sawyer locked the doors to her Mercedes SUV and headed for the main entrance of Kat's Got Your Tongue. She had no idea if the place was any good, but the name had caught her attention online. Hopefully, the food was as good as the play on words.

The delicious aroma of southern cooking and a soft jingle of bells greeted her as she stepped into the silver diner. It looked like something out of a nineteen-fifties movie. Taking in the *Seat Yourself* sign, Sawyer made her way to a booth along the front wall. Based on her phone's map, the diner sat in the heart of the small town of Carefree. Her home away from home for the next six weeks.

"Welcome to the diner." Sawyer turned away from the window to find a woman about her age laying a menu on the table. "Can I get you something to drink? You look like you could use something with a good kick, but unfortunately, I only serve some local beers and wine."

Did she look that rough? "Sweet tea will be fine."

"It's the hat and glasses." The server pointed in her direction as though she'd read Sawyer's mind. "You look like you either had a rough night or you're running from something. If you robbed the bank, just don't tell me. My husband's a sergeant with the CPD and happens to be sitting at the counter, so I'd be obligated to turn you in."

"No armed robbery," Sawyer laughed softly and slid her glasses off her face, careful not to make full eye contact. The last thing she needed was the server thinking she was here to rob the place. "More like a rough few months."

"In that case, I'll bring you a slice of my famous pecan pie on the house. It's good for the soul."

Before she could protest, the server turned and headed back to the counter. Sawyer's gaze followed the direction the woman was headed. Sure enough, seated at the bar was a man dressed in khakis and a navy polo shirt, with a badge and a gun clipped to his belt. Beside him, another man, dressed similarly in khakis and a white polo, was chowing down on a burger.

A loud grumble rolled through her stomach at the sight of food. She'd packed snacks for the road, but in her rush to get out the door without being seen, she'd forgotten the bag on her counter. And stopping had definitely been off the table. She hadn't wanted to risk anyone recognizing her at a gas station and posting it on social media.

Now that she had arrived in the quaint coastal town where her Christmas special was being shot, she would just have to roll the dice. It was only a matter of time before word got out in a community this small, but at least she would have her production team with her. On cue, her phone vibrated against the table as Stacy's picture appeared on the screen.

"Hey." Sawyer answered the phone, doing her best to sound cheerful.

"Just checking in on you. How much longer until you arrive?" Her show runner's voice was the epitome of calm, cool, and collected.

"Actually, I'm in town already. I stopped to grab something to eat before I headed to the inn."

There was a long pause. So much for being calm, cool, and collected. "Do you want me to send someone to meet you? Just tell me where you are."

That was the thing Sawyer loved about her team. Through everything, they stood by her. Well, maybe not Shaun given he'd just quit on her, but everyone else was rock solid. At least, she hoped they were. "I'm pretty sure I'm just around the corner at a place called Kat's Got Your Tongue, but I'm okay. The diner isn't super busy and I have my trusty no makeup-ball cap disguise on."

"I know the place, great food. Anyway, if you need me just text, I'll be there in five minutes tops. Oh, and by the way, we have a meeting with a local contractor this afternoon. Stella James, the lady that owns the place where you'll be staying, recommended him."

Sawyer breathed a sigh of relief. She may have been the brains behind the designs, but without a general contractor, they couldn't move forward on the project. Regardless of how much the show would be handling, it was a legal formality they couldn't skirt. Now all she had to do was turn on the charm and get the contractor to join the team, which usually wasn't very hard. People loved the idea of being a part of a TV show and the free advertising.

"What time is the meeting?" Sawyer glanced at her watch. It was already after one.

"Three o'clock, so you should have time to eat and you can freshen up at the inn."

Ending the call, Sawyer looked up to find the server was back with the sweet tea and promised pecan pie. "That looks amazing."

"Like I said, it's good for the soul." The server sat the plate on the table. "Sometimes you just need a little dessert first. Would you like to order something to go with the pie?"

"Actually." Sawyer glanced back to the two men sitting at the bar. "I'll have what he's having. That burger looks amazing."

The server took a quick glance in the direction of Sawyer's finger and smiled. "José, my cook, makes a mean bacon, cheddar, jalapeño burger. You picky about what comes on it?"

She didn't need the carbs or the heart attack, but what the hell. "No, whatever you want to put on it sounds good, I'm starving."

"My kind of girl." The server smiled. "I'm Kat by the way, the owner of this fine establishment. Welcome to Carefree. I have a feeling you'll fit in here just fine."

Sawyer's jaw dropped. "What makes you think I'm new here and not just a tourist on vacation?"

A devilish smile spread across Kat's lips. "Let's just say, I have a way of knowing things. It's sort of a superpower of mine. Also, I happen to know you're renovating the inn for a Christmas special, so you'll be around for at least a month or so. Of course, that's if you don't fall in love with our little town here and decide to stay longer."

Every muscle in Sawyer's body tightened at once. She'd been in town less than ten minutes and already someone recognized her.

Kat let out a soft chuckle. "Calm your horses. No one else has a clue who you are, and I'm not about to tell them."

"Why wouldn't you?" Sawyer's voice was colored with surprise.

Kat slid into the booth on the opposite side of the table. When she spoke again, her voice held a tighter tone. "I've been where you are. My ex, although he isn't quite as famous as yours, is an asshole with a capital A. I'm sure you've heard of him, Mark Hensley, *Georgia's next great governor.*"

Sawyer watched in surprise as the woman rolled her eyes, mocking the slogan of the Republican candidate. "You were married to Mark Hensley?"

"A long time ago, well before he got into politics, although I'm sure he's still just as much of an asshole. Anyway, the point is, I know how messy divorces can be. I can't imagine how much worse it would be with the tabloids airing every detail."

"You have no idea." Sawyer's head hung at the truth in her words.

"Well, consider this a safe space. I promise, no one will bother you here. And if they try, they'll have to answer to me. Now, I'll go put your order in so you can get to your meeting." Kat stood from the booth with a smile.

"Wait, how did—"

"I know things, remember. Total superpower."

For the first time in a very long time, Sawyer felt like a total stranger was on her side. The press had done their best to pose her as the villain in the failed fairy tale, but Kat had seen through the bullshit. Maybe things were starting to look up after all.

*****

Drew Scott sat at the counter of his sister's diner, regretting his latest life choice. Against his better judgement, he'd let his sister and soon-to-be sister-in-law talk him into a meeting with some production company out of Atlanta. The last thing he needed to add to his plate was an over-the-top renovation of the Saxton House Inn.

Truth be told, he'd never cared much for the home renovation shows. They were over produced and filled with unnecessary drama. Hell, the last time he'd bothered to watch one, he'd spent more time cussing their mistakes than enjoying any part of it. So why the hell he'd agreed to the meeting was the question of the year.

He didn't need the work. Scott Construction had more projects than they could get to as it was. Unfortunately for him, the women in his life seemed to have a way of talking him into poor choices.

Drew looked up from his burger as his sister, Kat, plated a piece of pie. "Just so you know, if this shit sinks my business, I'm moving into that apartment above your garage, rent free."

"You're such a baby." Kat shook her head as she set the plate down and poured a glass of sweet tea. "First of all, no one is forcing you to do it. And second, if your work is as good as you say it is, then you have nothing to worry about."

"My work is impeccable, but these shows are all about creating drama and shoddy craftmanship."

"Well, now they can have your drama and quality work. It'll be ground breaking."

Annoyed, Drew turned to Kat's husband sitting beside him at the bar. "How do you live with her?"

Before Marshall Brooks could answer, Kat pointed a finger at her husband. "Answer wisely, or you two will be sharing that garage apartment."

"Not a chance." Brooks laughed. "I've already taken my turn living up there. He can have it."

The garage apartment had been a revolving door for Drew's brothers and brother-in-law the last few years. First, his oldest brother Miles had lived there after returning home from a career in the service until he'd met his now wife, Julia. Brooks had done a short stint last year while he and Kat worked through the unplanned surprise that was Drew's niece. And earlier this year, their middle brother Liam had graced the apartment for a few weeks before rekindling things with his college sweetheart.

Now that Drew thought about it, maybe he should move in. It seemed to be the pathway to finding love. Not that he had time for dating, much less a wife. And adding a TV show to the mix definitely wasn't going to help in that department.

"All I'm saying is, I think this is a terrible idea, and I'm blaming Kat and Stella if the shit hits the fan."

A wicked smile spread across Kat's lips. "I think you'll be just fine."

Drew finished his lunch and spent the next thirty minutes taking up residence on the bar stool until Brooks had to return to work. Walking out to the back parking lot, Drew glanced at his watch. He still had an hour before he had to be at the Saxton House, which gave him just enough time to swing by the townhouses his crew was working on, and check in with the foreman.

Back in his truck, Drew had just rounded the corner, heading for the main exit when a loud crack echoed through the cab. Glancing in the driver's side mirror, he took in the sight of the black Mercedes pressed against his rear quarter panel.

"For fuck's sake." He threw the gear shift into park and climbed out of the truck.

"Oh my God, I'm so sorry."

Drew recognized the woman who'd been eating alone in the diner. Her ball cap was still in place, pulled incredibly low, but now she had on a pair of sunglasses that took up half her face. "That thing doesn't have a backup camera on it?"

Of course, maybe if you'd pull that hat up and remove those ridiculous glasses, you could see. He added to himself.

"It does, I guess I was just distracted."

Pulling his attention from the woman, Drew took in the damage. From best he could tell, it was mostly cosmetic. Squatting, he checked the wheel well to ensure nothing was rubbing the tire. All in all, it wasn't too bad. As for the Mercedes, however, the luxury SUV was going to need some TLC.

"My brother-in-law works for the CPD and just walked back across the street to the station. I can give him a call and have him come do a report."

"No!" The woman nearly screamed the word at him. "I'm sorry. I mean, I don't think that's necessary. The report. I can pay you. Whatever you think it's going to cost. Just give me a number."

What the hell was wrong with this woman? "That Mercedes won't be cheap to fix. You're going to want to file it with insurance, and last I checked, they'll want the police report."

"I'm not worried about my car. Just name your price." Her tone was full of irritation.

"Look lady, I'm just try—"

"Five thousand should cover it." The woman pulled a checkbook from her purse and began scribbling before he could finish his sentence.

"Whoa! That's way too much. My company has insurance to cover damages. I just have to pay the deductible."

"Well, consider the rest an inconvenience fee." She ripped the check from the book and pressed it against his chest.

Drew tried to make sense of the scene playing out before him. All he wanted to do was get the report so he could file the insurance. Obviously, if she could afford a Mercedes and to throw five grand around like it was nothing, she was doing better than him, but he would still need the report for his insurance.

"Look, I don't know what's going on, but my insurance company is still going to need the report." Drew gently grabbed her hand from his chest and pressed the check in her palm.

Pulling away, she let out a heavy sigh. "Then take the check and tell your brother-in-law it was a hit and run while you were in the diner. He can give you your report and my name doesn't have to be involved."

"You got some kind of warrant out for your arrest or something?" It was the only thing that made sense.

Pulling the sunglasses from her face, she looked up at him with sad eyes. "It's nothing like that. Please, just take the money and say you found it like this. Here, I can give you my number and if it costs more, I'll write you another check."

Before he could protest, she took his hand and began to scribble her phone number across his palm. When she was done, she placed the check back in his hand and closed his fingers around it. Drew glanced at the check and back to his truck. It was way too much, even without insurance, but there was a pleading to her voice that made him feel sorry for her.

Resigned, he shook his head and placed the check in his pocket. "Fine. If that's really how you want to play this, who am I to stop you?"

A gentle smile graced her lips. "Thank you."

"You're welcome, I guess." For the second time in a day, he'd let another woman convince him to do something he didn't think was the best idea. He was losing his edge. "Well, take it easy."

Back in his truck, Drew drove the short mile to where the townhouses were being constructed. Parking out front, he pulled the check from his pocket and stared at the name. Sawyer Linens. It sounded familiar, but he couldn't place it. Maybe she'd gone to Carefree High with them years ago? Or maybe he'd seen the name around town somewhere? Either way, he saved her name and number into his phone. Just in case, of course.

"What the hell happened to your truck?" Drew's foreman called through the open window.

Stepping out, he took another glance at the damage. "You wouldn't believe me if I told you."

To be continued...

Join my newsletter and follow me on Goodreads for updates on upcoming release.

Newsletter signup available at LeslieRayAuthor.com

Don't miss these great titles by Leslie Ray

The Carefree Series
EXPOSURE
UNEXPECTED
DIVISION
Book 4 (Coming Soon)
Book 5 (Coming Soon)

The Spruce Pine Series
RUN TO ME
FORGIVE ME

Follow me on social media
@LeslieRayAuthor

About The Author

Hi! If you haven't figured it out by now, I'm Leslie Ray, a small-town contemporary romance author. Born and raised in the South, I center my stories around all the wonderful memories of growing up in a small town in the southeast. When I'm not writing, you can find me hanging out with my homesteading husband, our two daughters (who mostly love each other), and our array of animals. When I've had enough of the sibling rivalry or the husband's canning, gardening, and chicken plucking, I love to mow. I can do amazing plotting spending hours on a mower.

Join me on social media to find out more!
Instagram @LeslieRayAuthor
Facebook @LeslieRayAuthor

Made in the USA
Columbia, SC
20 May 2023

17001106R00143